The Gift Horse

by

Charlie De Luca

© Charlie De Luca 2015

www.charliedeluca.co.uk

This is a work of fiction and any similarity to any persons living or dead is entirely coincidental.

To my family with love. x

Thanks for the following for their assistance;

Cover by Cresscovers.

Edited by My Cup of Tea Press

Many thanks to my clinical psychologist colleagues who provided me with detailed information on their work and training. Also, to my friends in racing who helped with my racing queries and police advisors too.

Chapter 1

It was a freezing, bitterly chilly day in November. The sort of day when you can see your breath and when anyone with any sense would be wrapped up by a warm fire. The sort of cold that seeps into your bones and no number of layers can prevent from taking a hold. Charlie Durrant was in the Weighing Room at Haydock Park, pulling on the bright purple, hooped colours of his favourite owner, Caroline Regan. At five feet ten inches, he was on the tall side for a jump jockey, but his endless legs and naturally high metabolism meant he could make the weights without too much trouble by missing the odd meal or having a sauna. Even so, today he was dreaming of a bacon sandwich and remembering the warmth of his bed.

'Penny for them? You look miles away,' commented his friend and fellow jockey Tristan Davies, as he adjusted his breeches. Tristan was as blond as Charlie was dark, but both were tall and rangy.

Charlie grinned. 'Nah, just thinking how I'm going to win and how delighted Caroline's going to be.'

There was a general murmur of ribald approval from the other jockeys about what form her gratitude might take. After all, it was not every day that you had a real life Bond girl turn up in the parade ring. She still caused a stir, even in her sixties.

'Bet she was a real looker in her day. She still is. And that voice...it's even on me satnav,' commented Jake Horton.

Caroline's trademark fruity, plummy voice was so well known that she was constantly in demand for voice overs, commercials and other products, even voiceovers on satnavs. She oozed charm and finesse. Charlie just hoped that her five year old grey gelding, Indian Ocean, called Indy for short, would be up to the two and a half mile trip and put in a good performance. He would hate to ruin her day.

Keith, the elderly valet coughed, pointedly looked at his watch and raised his eyebrows a fraction. The bell sounded right on cue.

'Come on then, lads. Let's get this show on the road.' Charlie scooped up his helmet and walked into the sunlight.

Caroline was wrapped in a huge fur coat which was topped off with a Russian style hat. She beamed at Charlie as he touched his cap. The parade ring was even more crowded than usual, all eyes trained on the delectable Miss Regan. When she pulled Charlie to one side, he smelt a waft of glorious, expensive scent and took in her smooth complexion, high cheekbones and Grecian nose.

'Do join me for a drink later Charlie, darling,' she whispered, her blue eyes twinkling. 'Win or lose. I want to speak to you about something...' Charlie was unable to ask her what she wanted to talk about, as the trainer, Miles Jamieson, took him aside for his instructions. He was youngish, in his late twenties and wore his blond hair in a floppy fringe style which gave him a foppish, academic air. It certainly belied his steely ambition. His father was **the** Nathaniel Jamieson, trainer to the Royals and all round master horseman. Having retired due to ill health, Miles was keen to live up to his father's reputation.

'Now then Charlie. Miss Regan is really hoping for a good result today and so am I. So, don't let Indy get ahead. Just hold him up and pick them off one by one in the last furlong or so. OK? From his last workout we should be in with a good chance. Just look out for Davies' mount, Benefactor, he's the one to watch. Got it? Splendid.'

Charlie nodded and was legged up onto the gorgeous looking, dappled grey horse. He did several more circuits of the parade ring, winked at Tristan Davies and looked his mount, Benefactor, up and down. He aimed to track this horse very carefully. The bay horse gleamed with condition and Charlie knew his trainer, Jeremy Trentham was bang on form. Although, he was best mates with Tristan, on the racecourse they were great rivals. He felt the familiar thrill of anticipation as his grey mount jogged excitedly. He had a race to win. He adjusted his racing goggles and kicked his mount into a canter as they made their way down to the start.

The field of twenty or so set off at such a lick that Charlie knew they would never sustain the pace. He had some difficulty coaxing the grey to settle down in midfield, but eventually managed it. He tracked Tristan on the bay, wearing red and yellow hooped colours and concentrated on positioning himself properly and staying out of trouble. Liam Docherty's mount, a huge chestnut gelding, pecked on landing over the fifth hurdle hurtling Liam to the ground. Charlie steered his mount away from the carnage of the fallen horse and Liam's small, curled up form. Charlie glanced briefly at the jockey, as the field all took steps to avoid crushing him. Damn. Falls were an everyday occurrence, but the camaraderie in the weighing room was such that everyone felt a wave a sympathy for fallers and wished them well. The field was beginning to thin, the early leaders starting to lose pace as they began the second circuit.

Indian Ocean was loving it. His blood was up, and he felt full of running as they leapt over hurdle after hurdle. He tried to hug the inside rail tracking Benefactor who was just ahead. Charlie quickly wiped his goggles and waited for the second last fence, before pulling out his right rein to position himself so that he could pass the big bay horse, who was running on well. He urged Indian

Ocean forward and gave him his head. The big grey needed no encouragement and pinged over the fence, landing just ahead of Benefactor. Tristan glanced at him and the two jockeys acknowledged each other briefly. It was a familiar enough scenario; a head to head battle between the two of them.

Charlie could hear the distant roar of the crowd as he urged his mount on, aware that Tristan was doing the same. They were just ahead as they came to the last and he pressed his legs against his mount, transferred his whip into his right hand and wafted it in Indian Ocean's eye line, just enough to get every last ounce of effort out of him. They sprang over the last fence with a massive leap, lengthening their lead. Benefactor wasn't done yet though, and Charlie could see the bay bravely trying to catch them. But the grey horse was full of running and gamely ran on to win by three or four lengths, cheered home by an ecstatic crowd. They had done it! Charlie caught his breath as he rode into the winner's enclosure to loud cheers and the white flash of camera bulbs. Miles clapped him on his back and Caroline gave him a huge hug and the steaming Indian Ocean, lots of kisses. He had forgotten how much press attention Caroline received as the crowd seemed denser than ever, all eyes trained on Miss Regan.

'Bloody well done,' exclaimed Miles clapping him on the back again. 'Well ridden.'

'You clever man!' exclaimed Caroline. 'I knew you'd do it. Don't forget to meet me for a drink after the last race. It's important.' Her blue eyes looked serious for a minute before a photographer called out to her and she posed for pictures, ever the true professional. Charlie wondered briefly what she wanted to speak to him about as she had mentioned it twice but was soon distracted by his preparations for the last race to give it any more thought.

He had a ride in the sixth race. Carnival was a chestnut gelding who he was riding for Owen Gleeson, a ruddy faced dairy farmer from Shropshire. The lanky four year old finished fifth which wasn't bad for his second race over hurdles, after a fairly undistinguished career on the flat. Owen's face lit up when Charlie explained the truth which was that he certainly had potential but was still rather green and had frozen a little when he was jostling for position amongst the other horses. Another problem had been a suspicious gurgling noise Carnival had made within the closing strides of the race, that suggested he had a soft palate. This was a potentially disabling condition where the horse swallows its tongue, struggles to breathe and gulps to try and right itself. Carnival had appeared to do this, then seemed to recover, but nevertheless it needed checking out. It was often one of the hardest parts of the job, to speak to owners about their horse's performance, particularly if it was disappointing. He spoke about tongue ties and other bits of tack that might help in the meantime but strongly urged a call to the vet. Eventually, when he had extricated himself, took some good natured ribbing from Tristan and the boys about his win, he joined Caroline Regan in her private box about an hour after the final race.

Caroline Regan was ensconced in her room overlooking the course, sitting by a radiator away from star struck punters. She had removed her fur hat revealing a chic blonde bob and had undone her coat showing her slim figure, which was encased in a clinging, knitted grey angora dress. She looked absolutely stunning, if not a little tiddly. There was a table laden with delicious nibbles and several empty bottles of champagne. Caroline appeared to have her own entourage. There was Miles, another man, who was suave and familiar looking with greying temples, who Caroline introduced as her friend and fellow actor, Robin Curtis and his homely looking wife, Lydia. There was also another distinguished looking man in his forties who she introduced as her son-in-law, bloodstock agent, Lawrence Prendergast.

Caroline fluttered her fingers at Charlie.

'Darling, you made it. Here he is everyone! You're so clever to have ridden dear Indy so well. Do have a drink.' Charlie helped himself to a champagne flute and exchanged half smiles with the others. Robin Curtis's wife, Lydia, looked him up and down. Judging from the look of them, they were all several drinks ahead of him.

'Aren't you rather tall for a jockey?' Lydia had grey almost blue, short hair and a rather lived in face. Her eyes, though, were grey and gleamed with intelligence. Charlie suspected she was Caroline's age but without the benefit of Botox or the surgery that he was sure enhanced Caroline's beauty. Albeit very skilfully, he had to admit.

'Oh, you don't need to be so lightweight for national hunt racing and I'm naturally pretty slim,' he explained.

Lydia nodded. 'So, you don't have to diet, then?'

Charlie smiled. 'Not as such, but I do watch what I eat and usually a sauna before the race does the job.'

Lydia gave him a wry smile. 'Lucky you. Well done today. You rode a good finish. I thought Trentham's horse might catch you at one point.'

'Hmm, not a chance,' muttered Lawrence Prendergast. 'His sire just isn't a stayer, you see. Knew he wouldn't go the distance.'

Miles looked at him in surprise. 'No, you're quite right. Whereas, Sea God, Indy's definitely is.'

Lawrence gave him a smile. 'I can see you are a fellow breeding enthusiast. It is vitally important to know your bloodlines, I find.'

'I couldn't agree more.'

Caroline rolled her eyes, patted the chair next to her and beckoned Charlie over.

'We'll leave you two to talk about breeding whilst I catch up with my favourite jockey.'

Charlie obediently sat down and listened whilst the others began discussing the merits of several different bloodlines.

Caroline lowered her voice and looked serious. 'Well, Charlie. I have a proposition to put to you. Now, I'm going to buy my granddaughter, Tara, a birthday gift. And I would really like you to assist her with it...'

Charlie's mind was in overdrive. What on earth was she suggesting? He had very little idea what went on in women's heads, never mind offering advice about what a spoilt, rich granddaughter of a former Bond girl might want for her birthday. He generally bought the woman in his life something quite simple, like a bottle of Chanel perfume and flowers. That usually did the trick.

'Well, I'm not sure about that, Caroline. Isn't there someone else who is better suited to advising your granddaughter? I'm sure you or your daughter will have much more idea than me.'

Caroline gave him a considering look. 'Now that's where you're wrong. You see, I intend to buy Tara a racehorse...'

'Right...' So that explained it. Lucky Tara.

Caroline watched his face. 'Don't you see? You will ride the creature, Miles will train it and Lawrence will oversee the purchase, of course. But you will be admirably suited to advising Tara and steering her through the minefield of being a racehorse owner.'

Charlie thought this through. Why was he admirably suited, any more than anyone else? Surely, Caroline had to have some sort of ulterior motive for her request? But for the life of him, he couldn't think what it could be. He racked his brains for a plausible excuse.

Caroline took another sip of champagne and studied him closely. She evidently took his silence as agreement.

'So, it's settled then.' This, Charlie couldn't help but notice, was more of a statement than a question. Caroline gave him her trademark Bond girl smile and tossed her head. 'Splendid, splendid, Charlie, darling.' She flapped her hand away, airily as though swatting away a tiresome fly. 'I'll be in touch with the details. Now, tell me all about Indy's race, won't you? I want to hear a blow by blow account.'

There seemed to be very little that Charlie could do after that but go along with Caroline's plan. Owners were king in the world of racing, as Miles was fond of reminding him. It would be rude not to help. After all, how difficult could it be?

Chapter 2

Tara Regan watched her client's face flush and then the tears started to fall. Ruth Cummings was a rather overweight, anxious woman in her forties, who kept anxiously clenching and unclenching her fists. She was agoraphobic and had been for several years. From the notes, it seemed that she had also been coming to the clinic on and off for several years, having seen a range of psychologists in that time. So, it had to be said that she had made little progress with her fears.

'You want me to walk with you outside as far as the gate?' repeated Ruth. Her face was etched with worry and misery and she was trembling uncontrollably. She was at the beginning of a full-blown panic attack, in fact.

Tara took all of this in but decided to press on anyway.

'Well, we have done the visualisation exercises for a couple of weeks now, so how do you feel about putting it into practice? I'll be with you every step of the way and we can take it as slowly as you feel you need to. If you feel more acute symptoms coming on, then we can pause and either go on or come back. It's up to you... But remember the panic will start to subside.'

Ruth was struggling to breathe and compose herself. Tara didn't want to instantly back down and suggest that they go back to the visualisation again. She had to push her, just a little out of her comfort zone, but not so she was absolutely frozen in terror. However, Ruth appeared to be crumbling before her eyes. She abstractly plucked at her tweed skirt and crossed and recrossed her legs. Her complexion was becoming more and more pallid and she looked utterly terrified. She was perched on the edge of her seat, her hands flickering with tension, as though she wanted to make a run for it. She probably did, as the fight and flight hormone adrenaline had definitely kicked in.

Tara paused waiting for her to come to a decision for herself.

Ruth looked as though she was having an inner battle with her demons and was uncertain what to do next.

'Right,' Ruth stood up and walked briskly towards the door. She slowed down at the last minute and turned to Tara, her lips trembling. 'No, no. You know, I can't do it. I just can't do it today...' Ruth's voice was high and then she began crying again, silent tears at first followed by great wracking sobs. Tara handed her the tissue box she always kept handy and waited. She wasn't about to give up quite so easily.

'Well, it's clear that you're still highly anxious, but if we just take it one step at a time. Remember the five R's we spoke about last week? React, retreat, relax, recover and repeat? Well, you are in the react phase and we need to get you to retreat and relax and then repeat. Just take a deep breath, breathe in for the count of seven and out for the count of eleven....'

Ruth looked undecided and then walked back away from the office door, shaking her head.

'No, no I just can't do it. There's no way...'

Tara paused. 'OK, that's absolutely fine...'

Ruth wiped her nose and gave Tara a grateful look. Tara instantly felt as though she had capitulated too easily and that perhaps should have let the fight and flight reaction start to wane before pushing her just a little. Damn.

'It's just with everything, I can't face it today... You do understand?' Ruth continued.

Tara nodded and remembered to keep her posture open and not show any of the frustration she was feeling. She took a deep breath.

'Absolutely, it was just a suggestion, but of course we have to go at your pace. And if you want to leave it, then that is absolutely fine. We'll try again next week. Shall we make another appointment?'

Ruth smiled and seemed a great deal calmer, even managing a slight smile. Tara fished in her bag for her diary and they made another time to meet next week.

'I'll just ring Dave so he can come and fetch me,' Ruth muttered, rummaging in her bag for her mobile 'phone. They said their goodbyes and minutes later Tara observed from the window, as Dave pulled up directly outside in his white fiesta and helped Ruth negotiate the few steps to his car. Tara noticed Ruth's white face as she hesitated and then rushed to the safety of the car in one deft, accomplished movement. Perhaps, she could use Dave in the sessions? Tara wondered if it was handy to have your husband at your beck and call whenever you needed him and whether this was why the phobia persisted? After all, there must be some pay off for her behaviour, something positive that came out of it, otherwise why would it be so resistant to change? Then she chided herself for her lack of generosity. It had seemed so much easier in the lectures, Tara realised, but then she hadn't considered the difficulties of putting theory into practice with real people with real problems. It almost made her long for the haven of the lecture theatres and seminar groups.

Tara was twenty five and undertaking her postgraduate training, a doctorate in Clinical Psychology. This was a course run jointly but the Universities of Hull and York. She was in her second year which was split between placements and lectures. She had already completed several placements but this one, working with adults, was proving the most demanding. She made a note in her diary to talk to her supervisor, Jack Ferguson, about the slow progress of Ruth Cummings, not necessarily within her sessions but overall. She had been coming for help for several years with almost no progress. Perhaps, she needed to think of another approach? She glanced at her watch. It

15

was almost five and time to go home. She typed up her case notes and then shut down her computer, her thoughts turning to tonight when she was meeting Callum. She felt a shiver of anticipation.

Tara shook her head, as if trying to dismiss the thought of Callum and Anna together. She ought to follow her own advice and principles of cognitive behavioural therapy and change her thinking. Tara pictured her and Callum together with Alfie, sometime in the future, all happy and relaxed. She was sure that Anna would need the creases in her and Callum's separation to be ironed out before allowing Alfie to stay with them. And that could take months, she decided. She would enjoy the role of a sort of stepmother, she knew. But for now, she should just enjoy the relationship, go with the flow and see where things went.

She had a party planned the following weekend, which would be a family and friends affair hosted by her glamorous grandmother, Caroline Regan. So that was another thing to look forward to and as she hadn't yet introduced Callum to her family, it suited her perfectly. They sort of knew she was seeing someone, but she had been vague about any details. When she analysed things, she wasn't quite sure why she hadn't told her family anything much about Callum. Perhaps, she just didn't want to jinx the relationship, or maybe she didn't want to explain about Callum's separated but still married status? Caroline, she knew, would take it all in her stride, but she wasn't at all sure about her parents' reaction if she was brutally honest. The divorce would happen, but before that there was bound to be some grey areas. Being candid, Callum's marital status did make her feel rather like a scarlet woman and a marriage wrecker. The thought of Alfie desperately missing his father made her feel even worse. Despite Callum's rosy view that everything would work out in the end, she had to admit that she still had some reservations.

However, the thought of her party and her grandmother made her smile. Charming and still stunning with that famous plummy voice, Caroline Regan, had offered to throw her beautiful country house open to host the birthday party for her. Tara adored her, but also realised that her father and her aunt had struggled in their childhood as a direct result of being the daughter of a glamorous Bond girl and all round British icon. Having an actress as a mother was not always conducive to stable child care arrangements and her father, Jack and his sister Lola, were shunted from place to place and had really struggled when their parents had finally separated after several reconciliations. Such instability led Jack, her father, to eschew such a lifestyle and he had gone into a profession as far away from the uncertainty and glamour of acting as he could possibly think of. He had become an accountant and enjoyed the absolute certainty of dealing with figures which were constant and above all predictable.

He was determined that his own children should have the stability his own childhood lacked and married her mother, Kate, who was a teacher. She had no qualms about giving up her career as soon as Tara, and then her brother Fraser arrived. Despite Tara's stable childhood, it was probably her father's description of his, that had made her study Psychology. She had a fascination with the inner workings of the human mind and enjoyed probing its inner recesses. Her aunt, Lola, had also rejected a thespian lifestyle and married a Bloodstock agent, Lawrence Prendergast. She lived a contented life in the country in a vast house with lots of horses and dogs. Only her brother Fraser wanted to follow in his grandmother's footsteps and had gained a place at the prestigious acting school at the Royal Academy, much to her grandmother's approval.

Caroline, she knew had not intended to harm her own children in anyway, but fame had its drawbacks. Her relationships were constantly dissected by the media and both her children were endlessly scrutinised and exposed. Caroline was aware of this and as a result spent a great deal of time fussing and worrying over her grandchildren, as if to compensate. Tara loved her grandmother; they got on famously. However, Caroline didn't understand her granddaughter's choice of career and had expressed her worries about Tara's 'seriousness'. Caroline felt that she just didn't have enough fun in her life. She was, therefore, no doubt considering how to remedy this and would have bought Tara an expensive and frivolous birthday present. As she had impeccable taste, Tara felt a frisson of excitement, as she pondered what this might be.

Back home, Tara caught up with her housemates, Emily and Gabriella over a cup of tea. They had been living together for a couple of years now. After she had shaken of the stresses of the day, she decided to get ready for her date. She chose a red figure hugging shift dress, heels, hastily applied mascara and lip gloss and ran a brush through her shoulder length, layered conker brown hair. She topped it off with a squirt of Chanel Number 5, grabbed her long, wool coat and stepped out into the chilly night.

Chapter 3

Charlie urged Zorba the Greek, his bay horse, forward onto the gallops at the stables. As the stable jockey, Charlie often took part in the work riding at home and was keen to try Zorba out. Let's see what you can really do, he thought, as he gave Zorba his head and pressed his legs against the horse's sides. Zorba accelerated and started to move ahead of his training companions. He left them standing and one of them was Clair de Lune, a stunning black horse who had won a couple of selling plates. These were races at the lower end of the racing spectrum where the winner was auctioned at the end of the race, although the yard could buy the horse back if they wished. Racecourses were keen to run these as they earned a percentage of the selling price, but also it gave less talented horses the opportunity to win against modest competition. So at least he had a realistic yardstick in terms of Zorba's ability and it told him Zorba had real speed, as Clair de Lune was left standing. Charlie felt the sheer acceleration of the horse and exhilaration coursed through him. God, he had real scope. Having schooled Zorba over hurdles a few times, he knew he had a great jump too. If he had the stamina and only time would tell, they could have a real contender on their hands. Charlie began to pull up as they approached their makeshift winning post and tried to suppress his excitement. Zorba felt full of running and had barely broken into a sweat, even though this was their third circuit. He waited for the other horses and work riders to join him, wiped his goggles and tried to stop smiling. All five horses and riders turned and made their way back to Miles, who was sitting in his Land Rover, his window down whilst he trained his binoculars on them.

'OK, lads, that's enough for today. Make your way back, will you?' Miles glanced briefly at Charlie, his expression quizzical. 'Well?'

Charlie took off his goggles and looked at Miles' expectant face.

'Bloody brilliant turn of speed. If he has the stamina, then he could be one of the best...'

Miles nodded, a triumphant smile playing at his lips.

'Thought so. Fantastic! Meet you back at the house for a drink?'

Charlie gave him the thumbs up and allowed Zorba, who was keen to catch up with the other horses, his head. He absently patted Zorba's well muscled neck and allowed him to trot on, his body rising rhythmically in the saddle.

It was a cold, but clear November morning and there was a hint of sunshine as they rode back to the house. Charlie was the back marker and half listened to the chatter of the other lads, pulled up his collar and reflected on the season ahead. Miles Jamieson was an up and coming trainer, who had learned his trade with his father, Nathaniel. He had been something of a legend in racing circles. After his retirement due to ill health, he and his wife had downsized and moved into a cottage in a nearby village and Miles had taken over the stables and house at Thornley. Thornley was in a delightful rural spot close to the racing town of Walton in North Yorkshire and the village edged onto ancient woodland which was picturesque, with its sheltered trails, that were fantastic for short gallops and training runs.

Charlie was twenty-six and had been a conditional jockey to Nat Jamieson for whom he had the greatest of respect. He had been made stable jockey a couple of years ago and had been given a nearby cottage to live in. Nat has struggled with a heart problem so had retired last season. His son, Miles had given up his job as a land agent to take over the running of the yard. Generally, he got on well with Miles and realised that he was keen to succeed. Underneath the floppy fringe, traditional clothes and diffident manner, lay a determination to prove himself. With Nat acting in an advisory role, he was sure that he would succeed, especially with Miles bringing lots of modern technology and ideas to the sport. He had installed a swimming pool for the horses, monitored their heart rates and took lots of other measurements, whereas his father relied on common sense and instinct to assess a horse's fitness. Nat grumbled about Miles' methods but between them he felt they offered a unique blend of the old and the new, which should reap dividends.

Charlie was looking forward to the season ahead. He loved racing, enjoyed the camaraderie in the weighing room and the thrill of winning made him feel quite euphoric. He was confident and generally happy go lucky most of the time. With his handsome features, thick dark hair and blue eyes, fringed with dark lashes, he was not short of female admirers and his increased success in terms of racing and the corresponding rise in his media profile, had helped. He had even been featured in one paper as one of the hunkiest national hunt jockeys in the run up to the Grand National. Sadly, his horse fell at Beecher's, but it had led to lots of female attention. For now, he was happy to play the field. Sometimes, he thought he wasn't ready for a long term relationship. Maybe, he didn't feel he deserved it after what had happened? His mind flitted back to that terrible day and he recognised that familiar dread that pulled him down. Fortunately for him, his stream of consciousness was interrupted by Zorba shying, as a bird flew out of the copse.

'Give over, you daft bugger,' he muttered to Zorba as he regained his balance. He could have been speaking to himself because he knew only too well that it did not do to dwell on the past. He must focus on his bright future, instead.

Thornley House was a stone farmhouse set slightly back from the main yard, where there were fifty or so stables. The horse walker and horse swimming pool were located prominently and there was even a solarium. Since his father's retirement there had been a few mutterings from loyal owners whose opinion was divided on Miles' prowess as a trainer. Of course, he had learned a great deal from the old man when he was growing up, but a fascination with science and a spell at Agricultural College led him to have a great interest in how science could be applied to farming, animal husbandry and now racing. Some of the criticisms Charlie had heard were about the fact that Miles had much less natural affinity for the horses than his father had, but whether the appliance of science would make up for this or even help him surpass his father's achievements, only time would tell. For now, the owners seemed to be happy enough to give Miles his head, despite some misgivings.

Charlie untacked Zorba, ran a brush over him and examined the beautiful bay with a critical eye. His conformation was perfect. He had a wide muscled chest, straight legs and a calm temperament to boot, which made him very trainable. Charlie fished into his pocket and gave the horse a polo mint. Zorba crunched it loudly and then nudged Charlie roughly with his head, keen for another one.

'Oh, go on then, just one more then that's your lot.' Charlie patted the silky forelock between the horse's ears. He lifted it and noticed that Zorba had a double whorl, two crowns where the hair grew in a circle, close together. It was unusual, and he remembered an old head lad he used to work with and all round horseman, Jack Farnham, telling him that the double whorl combination between a horse's eyes, was a sure sign of a good horse. Well, he was certainly right in Zorba's case. He had very high hopes of him.

Will Mellor, the Head Lad came up to chat to him. He was in his forties and was very experienced. He had started out as a stable lad under Nathaniel and the general view was that what he didn't know about horses, wasn't worth knowing. He also worked very long hours, more so since his wife had left him, taking his two young children with her. Will had been drinking more heavily and was often spotted in The Yew Tree pub in Walton propping up the bar trying to drown his sorrows. However, he ran the yard like clockwork and his work, at least, had not slipped.

'How's it going, Will?' Charlie gave him a sympathetic look.

'Oh, you know, so so. The missus is being awkward about me seeing the kids. But mustn't grumble. I daresay it'll sort itself out.' Will shook his head and gave a wry smile. Charlie remembered his wife, Linda. She had seemed like a straightforward, reasonable sort of a woman. How had things gone so wrong, he wondered?

'Anyway, I've a bone to pick with you, losing me my best Travelling Head Girl...'

Charlie grimaced. Gina. He had been having an on off relationship with her, but she had been very upset when Charlie ended things a few weeks ago, so much so, she had threatened to leave. He hadn't realised she was serious. Charlie felt rather sad and very guilty that she was leaving. Perhaps, he should try to talk to her?

'Yeah, sorry about that. I didn't think she'd actually hand in her notice.'

'Well, you never can tell what a woman will do.' Will screwed up his weather-beaten face. He made it sound like the opposite sex were a complete mystery to him. 'Anyway, the guvnor will be appointing someone soon, but they'll have some big boots to fill.'

'Yes, they will. I'll maybe have a word with her,' Charlie suggested, appalled.

Will nodded. 'Yes, you do that, Charlie. You never know it may do the trick.'

Miles looked up from his laptop as soon as Charlie arrived. Sitting with him was the yard vet, Roger King. Roger was in his fifties, grey haired and kindly. He had been the yard vet for many years. He was known for being very thorough, a little over cautious but had many years of experience monitoring equine health to call upon.

'Right, tea?' Miles stood up and began washing up mugs. Charlie acknowledged Roger and took in the surroundings. Since Miles had taken over, all his time seemed to be spent on researching scientific facts and he never seemed to notice that things needed cleaning and tidying up. Glancing through the open door to the kitchen, the sink was full of dirty pots and the surfaces full of empty take away packages, and the aroma of stale curry was pervasive. His mother, Prue, who cooked like a dream and kept the farmhouse immaculate, would have been mortified. Another consideration was that most training yards had an open house on certain days, such as Sunday for owners to come and see their horses and discuss their progress with the trainer. Nat and Prue had managed this brilliantly as Prue always baked beautiful cakes and kept the house immaculate. Owners who couldn't manage visits on a Sunday, were free to visit by arrangement. Either way, the house should be kept clean and tidy at all times. Charlie knew it would be bad for business if standards were not maintained.

'Hey mate, you need a cleaner or a wife. Whatever happened to Isabella, was it?' quipped Charlie.

Miles' face clouded as he deposited three mugs of tea on the table, half spilling the contents.

'Well, let's just say we are no longer an item. And yes, I am in the process of employing a cleaner since girlfriends can be so bloody unreliable.'

Roger and Charlie exchanged a look. Clearly things hadn't ended well for Miles and his rather posh girlfriend, Isabella Forbes. Shame, she had rather a good sense of humour and tended to call a spade a spade. Charlie had rather liked her.

'So, what happened?'

Miles shrugged. 'She went off with a richer guy...'

'Right... Ouch...'

Roger got to his feet, looking awkward. It was clear that he wanted to make himself scarce. He was of the generation that was embarrassed by soul searching or male bonding.

'OK then. I'll ask Monsoon's lad to help me. You two carry on and chat.'

Miles waited for Roger to leave and ran his fingers through his floppy fringe.

'I'm thinking of getting another vet in. What do you think? Someone more up to date and modern. Old King's methods went out with the ark. He just suggested box rest for a pulled tendon yet modern technology like PEMF can vastly accelerate healing greatly. I'm not sure he's even heard of it.'

Charlie looked bewildered. He wasn't sure he had either.

'It's Pulsed Electromagnetic Fields therapy and it works wonders in promoting the healing of soft tissue injuries. Haven't you heard of it?'

'No, yes...I'm just surprised about Roger. Your father swore by him.'

Miles shook his head. 'But you've got to admit, he is a bit of a fossil.'

Charlie shrugged. 'But he has a vast amount of experience too.' Charlie felt some sort of loyalty to the man, having worked with him for a few years. He was extremely good with the horses and was a reliable and trustworthy professional.

Miles took a slurp of tea and warmed to his theme. 'I've already spoken to someone Lawrence Prendergast suggested, a young vet called Alistair Morgan who is making quite a name for himself. He's bang up to date with every scientific development there is.'

Charlie nodded. 'Right, well it's up to you, I suppose.'

Miles grinned and opened his laptop. 'And we have a new travelling head lad. Obviously with Gina leaving I have had to appoint someone else...'

Charlie grimaced. Gina. 'Yes, I've just been speaking to Will about her. Do you think if I had a word, she may change her mind? I didn't expect her to hand in her notice.'

Miles smiled kindly. 'Well, it's a bit late for that, I'm afraid. She's gone. She had some leave owing and so she's not going to be coming back. Look, she didn't want me to tell you.'

'Right. I'm sorry.' Charlie took this in. He couldn't get over the fact that she had left without so much as a word. He tried to analyse his feelings. He wished now that he had been able to speak to her, ask her to stay. He was sure they could have still worked together somehow. He felt a real heel that she had to leave a job that she loved, just because of him. And she was an excellent Travelling Head Girl too. Will would be devastated, he realised. It occurred to him that they were all quite useless with women, Will, Miles, himself. Perhaps, it was the job, the long hours or something?

'Well, never mind. I have appointed someone called Mick Richards, as Travelling Head Lad, who comes very highly recommended. He's starting in a few days so don't worry and frankly he has far more progressive ideas than Gina. Now, let's get on with these entries, then shall we?' Miles rubbed his hands together and beamed. 'You know what, I think we're going to have an excellent season, don't you, especially with the likes of Zorba and owners like Caroline Regan and her granddaughter. And with the new vet, Alistair, and the new lad on board, we could really go places.'

Charlie nodded, trying to look positive and 'progressive.'

'Has Caroline's son-in-law come up with a horse for her granddaughter yet?'

'I'm not sure, but he's certainly in the right job. That reminds me,' he tapped away on his computer. 'Both you and I are invited to Caroline's granddaughter's birthday party. She sent me an email. I'll print off the invitation and directions for you. She managed to prise your telephone number out of me too. She obviously doesn't trust me to tell you. Look...' He turned the laptop towards Charlie.

Charlie nodded and tried to concentrate on the computer screen. Miles pressed print and picked up the sheet that the printer spat out and handed it to Charlie, who pocketed it absently. He couldn't help but feel rather shocked and hideously guilty about Gina's departure and with Roger being replaced too, he was starting to feel a little uneasy. Would he be traded in for a more up to date, progressive model too?

Chapter 4

Tara luxuriated in the warmth of her bed and turned over expecting to find the solid mass of Callum at the other end of her duvet. Her hand momentarily searched, fingers stretching out into nothingness. Then the horrible realisation flooded through her. Her head was pounding, and she felt she had grit in her eyes, as she tried to remember. She had the sinking, guilty feeling that she had behaved badly, as she pieced together the fragments of her memories of last night. It had all started off so well. She had met Callum at Al Fresco, an expensive French restaurant. He had looked divine in his best grey suit, crisp white shirt and smelt of some fabulous musky yet citrus scent. His collar length dark curls had looked especially sexy and his hazel eyes had been full of love. She remembered the beautifully wrapped gift he had presented her with, and the thrill of opening the trademark sky blue box containing a fabulous Tiffany bangle, whilst they sipped champagne and ordered a sumptuous feast. Somewhere between the starter and the main course, Callum had started to receive text messages on his phone and although he had manfully ignored them initially, they had become more and more insistent.

The beautiful, intimate mood had finally been broken once and for all when Anna has eventually rang him saying that Alfie had been admitted to hospital with suspected meningitis, at which point a sorrowful, apologetic Callum, had kissed her, begged forgiveness, but hightailed off to the local infirmary, leaving her sitting picking over her meal, trying not to notice the pitying glances from the waiters and other guests.

Then, she had arrived home, promptly drank an entire bottle of champagne bought especially, chucked the bangle on her dressing table and had a good weep. Still not feeling any better, she had found a bottle of whiskey and had had a few glasses of that too. The worst thing was, and this caused her the most pain, although her evening was ruined, she found she was quite disgusted and ashamed of herself, because she was jealous of Alfie. There, she had admitted it. Fancy being jealous of a small boy? She was ashamed of herself and how spoilt and pathetic that made her feel. At least she hadn't been too sniffy with Callum and had managed to swallow her true feelings and think about Alfie, but there was this small but insistent voice that kept asking if she could really cope with a man with a child and all that would entail? And more importantly, could she cope with the irrational and jealous person it had turned her into? She buried her head under the covers and tried to block out the sickly, guilty feelings this generated.

Several hours later, she was dressed, sitting eating toast with her housemate Gabriella and trying to keep down a cup of tea.

'Well, you couldn't exactly expect him to carry on eating his meal when he heard about Alfie being admitted to hospital, surely?'

Tara took another bite of toast and chewed thoughtfully. 'No, of course not. I was just disappointed and bloody well pissed off, that was all.'

Gabriella shook her head. 'Well, I hope you didn't actually say that, I mean you knew he had a child when you went out with Callum. What did you expect…?'

'No, no of course I didn't say anything. He didn't really give me much chance, anyway. But he's not even going to be there for my party because he has a pre-booked holiday with Alfie, so I'm just annoyed that's all… I mean he's working very hard and can't always come around, then there's his family commitments and other excuses. I don't know, I just feel like it's going nowhere.'

Gabriella gave her a severe look, as she stirred her tea.

'Look, do you think he's not actually separated, or maybe secretly wanting to patch things up with Anna? I presume you are sure everything is resolved between them? I mean have you actually been to his place?'

'Yes, of course I have.' Tara tried to think back to her last visit. Callum's current relationship with Anna was something she had worried about, but she thought she had read the clues well. And when given the opportunity, she had had a bloody good look around Callum's flat. Any self respecting woman would have done the same, she told herself. She had looked in the bathroom cabinet, delved into Callum's chest of drawers and found not so much as a stray toothbrush. His flat was exceptionally tidy, though, as if he had given it a really good spring clean. Again, that was normal behaviour for a man expecting a woman to visit, wasn't it? He was trying to impress her. Of course, she had considered all the signs and there wasn't even so much as a sniff that his ex had been there.

'No, you're barking up the wrong tree,' she continued, with rather more confidence than she felt. Gabriella ran her fingers through her thick, blonde mane.

'Well, if you haven't argued, there's no harm done, is there? And besides he's not coming to your proper party where your amazing grandmother is bound to have invited some hot single guys, so you have a plan B. What's the problem?'

Tara shrugged and finished off her toast. Trust Gabriella to put things into perspective.

'Well, there isn't one.'

Gabriella smiled, encouragingly. 'That's my girl.' Except unbeknown to her, Gabriella had touched a raw nerve and Tara indulged herself in prodding around it. Supposing Callum was cherishing the belief that he would get back together with Anna? Perhaps, Tara was just an 'OK for now' sort of a girlfriend whilst he waited for Anna to change her mind? One thing was for sure, with all this uncertainty she really had to ask herself, did she really know Callum Taylor as well as she thought she did? Or herself for that matter.

Sunday lunch was the usual cosy affair. Tara's family lived in a beautiful country house in rural Yorkshire, in Market Leighton not far from York. Her father had decided to remedy his own rather rootless and insecure upbringing which resulted from being Caroline Regan's son. So, he and her mother had succeeded in creating a lovely, homely environment for their children, Tara and her brother, Fraser. Their mother, Kate had initially trained as a teacher but gave it up as soon as Tara was born because her father had made a real success of his accountancy job, so she hadn't needed to work. She busied herself by tending her wonderful, traditional garden, cooking, fussing round her father and sitting on various local committees, including being the Chair of Governors at the local Secondary School. She was an excellent and accomplished cook. After a lovely lunch of beef wellington, served with roast parsnips, carrots and sweet potatoes, followed by apple pie and custard, her mother cleared away the plates and made a coffee.

'So, darling. Are you looking forward to your birthday party?' Kate asked.

Her father looked up from the Sunday papers and rolled his eyes at the mention of the party. Tara ignored him.

'Yes, I'm sure it will be lovely. It's good of Granny to let us have the party at her house, isn't it?'

There was a rustle of newspaper and her father's face appeared over the top, scowling again. He adored his mother but hadn't quite forgiven her for the time she had devoted to her career when he was a boy. Consequently, he had a hatred of 'luvies' as he called them. He indulged Fraser's interest in acting and regarded it as a mere whim that wasn't likely to be successful. It was a shame really, because Fraser showed real flair and a steely determination to succeed.

Her father continued to scowl. 'Well, that's because, she can invite who she likes. She's bound to have invited half the luvies in England.'

Her mother gave him a baleful look. 'You know you'll enjoy it when you get there, Jack. You always do.' This was certainly true. Tara remembered him bopping away to some disco classics when he had sunk a pint or two at her last birthday bash.

He sighed. 'Well, when it comes to Ma, what I do know is that she never does anything without good reason. She's bound to have some ulterior motive. She's probably lined up some bloke or other that she wants to set Tara up with. Just hope he's not a bloody thespian.'

Tara found her grandmother's preoccupation with her love life quite amusing. Perhaps, judging by the current state of her relationship with Callum, it might even be a good thing. She hadn't heard anything from Callum, despite sending him a neutral sounding text message asking after Alfie. She shook her head trying to work out what it all meant? Maybe, something terrible had happened and they were sitting at hospital, ashen faced, waiting for news? Perhaps, Alfie was absolutely fine, but the potentially life threatening event could have reunited Callum and Anna? Worries spun round and round her head and gnawed away at her.

'Well, I agree it's a lovely idea,' replied her mother, taking in Tara's pale and anxious appearance. Tara noticed the look and deliberately plastered on a smile. Any minute she would be asking her if she was eating properly, so she tried to pre-empt her, and forced herself to stop ruminating over Callum. She knew she was not looking her best and probably the alcohol she had necked had made her paranoid.

'Darling, you are eating properly, aren't you? Only you look rather pale,' continued her mother.

Tara smiled. 'Course, I'm eating fine. You worry too much.'

'And your doctorate, I hope that's going alright?'

'Yes, it's fine, honestly. Challenging work but it's going well.'

Her father glanced at her and stroked his chin. He continued to wrestle his paper into submission, a slight smile playing on his lips.

'I wonder what this year's frivolous and totally useless gift will be? What do you think, Kate? Honestly, Ma really spoils you and Fraser. Do you remember the acres of the moon she bought you when you were three, or the original 'Star Wars' Jedi mask she bought Fraser? And the rest?' Her father scratched his head and smiled indulgently. 'What about you the diamond bracelet when you were nine or the invite to the premiere of The Return of 007? Honestly, I ask you?' There was pride and exasperation, all mingled together in his tone.

Tara certainly did remember. She still treasured that diamond bracelet. They hadn't known that the diamonds were real, and she was in the habit of wearing the bracelet to school, until her parents realised and wrestled it from her. She was the envy of all her friends having been to the premiere and dined with Pierce Brosnan himself, had a collection of divine, designer handbags and a wardrobe of the latest must haves. There had been countless splendid birthdays treats including her grandmother hiring out Alton Towers for the day, tea at Claridge's, a brand new Mini on her seventeenth birthday, a designer ball gown for her Prom and a trip to New York when she graduated. Then she remembered her grandmother's appearances at school plays, charming the dour and irritable head teacher, Mr Hadley, and applauding loudly at her mediocre performances. Everyone had wanted to be her friend and their mothers were anxious to find out Caroline's beauty secrets, whilst the fathers gasped and practically fell at her feet. Caroline Regan entranced and charmed people at will and her presence had enhanced Tara's life. She really was like a real life fairy grandmother turning up and dispensing beautiful gifts, glamour and good humour with a wave of her magic wand. And Tara adored her.

Her mother gave her father a worried look.

'Well, don't look at me. I don't know what she's got planned. You know how she likes surprises. I haven't heard so much as a whisper but knowing Caroline, I'm sure the year's gift will be just as glamorous and unsuitable as all the others. And, no doubt, you'll be thrilled with it.'

Charlie was riding at Wetherby where Miles had a couple of runners and he had picked up two more rides from another local trainer, Laura Palmer. Wetherby was their local course being situated between York and Leeds and Charlie had ridden many winners there, so had a great affinity with the place. He was riding Clair de Lune, Miles' black gelding that had won a couple of selling plates and Fringe Benefits, a bay horse for a new owner in the third and had a couple of rides in the fourth and the fifth race. As he changed into the purple colours of Clair de Lune's syndicate, he listened to his friend Tristan Davies' chatter. Tristan had, with the help of a stable lad, Kyle Devlin and Tristan's girlfriend Poppy, foiled a complex betting scam that involved the mafia and a mathematical genius of an owner, who had devised a complex betting system involving multiple bets on talented but little raced horses, in order to scoop millions. That was the plan anyway, until Tristan and Poppy had worked out what was going on and involved the authorities. Two jockeys, Melvin Clough and Marcus Eden were currently suspended pending police and British Horseracing Authority inquiries, and it had sent shock waves through the racing community. Most jockeys were completely honest, if not a bit mad, and were glad when any bad apples were brought to justice, as otherwise it reflected badly on the sport. The jockeys generally heard whispers of illegal goings on, which were based on truth more often than not. However, it was often a different matter finding hard evidence, that was the problem.

'So, the mafia were alive and well, in Yorkshire? God, who would have thought it! Still, I'm not sorry about Cloughie, he was always a miserable sod and we all knew he was a bit dodgy.' Charlie grimaced at the thought of Cloughie's dishonesty. 'I didn't suspect Marcus Eden, though, I must say.'

'Nor me,' continued Tristan. Marcus was a relative newcomer and had seemed pleasant enough. 'It just goes to show, doesn't it?'

Another young jockey, Joel O'Neill's ears pricked up. 'It goes to show what? What are you two gossiping about?' He was a nice enough lad, but rather inquisitive with dark hair and sticky out ears to boot, which appeared to have given him the hearing ability of a bat.

'Just talking about your chances, Joel. That's all. We don't fancy yours much,' quipped Charlie.

'Yeah, Captain Fantastic is a real misnomer,' continued Tristan, in the same vein, dismissing Joel's ride.

Joel's face fell until he caught the wink that Charlie gave Tristan.

He grinned back and then turned away, his face colouring when another jockey Derek Jones came into the Weighing Room.

Tristan and Charlie exchanged a look. Derek was a reasonable jockey but known for chasing rides in a rather an aggressive manner assisted by his rather sharp agent, Tony Ross. His agent had the habit of ringing trainers and suggesting that other jockeys were going to other race meetings and couldn't possibly make it in time to ride their horse. Having planted the seed of doubt, Tony would ring the trainers frequently, explaining that Derek was still available. If they hadn't heard from other agents by then, they had been persuaded to book Derek just to be on the safe side, only to leave their usual jockey annoyed and disappointed when their agents finally rang to confirm their availability. Charlie wondered if Joel had lost rides because of him? Derek had been mainly working in the Epsom area previously but had come up north in the last few months where he was swiftly getting himself a rather dubious reputation.

He was a rather slim individual, with bleached blond hair and blue eyes that slightly protruded. He also had an obsequious manner, that belied his thinly veiled ambitions. He reminded Charlie of a reptile for some reason.

'Now then gentlemen, how's tricks?' Derek rubbed his hands together, eager eyes darting from Charlie to Tristan. 'I haven't had the pleasure of making your acquaintance,' he continued with exaggerated politeness. He extended a pale hand to Charlie who shook it doubtfully. His hand was cold and clammy to the touch and Charlie had to fight the urge to wipe his fingers on his breeches afterwards. Tristan appeared to be similarly reluctant to shake his hand.

'I hear that you gentlemen are the ones to beat,' Derek continued, smiling in his reptilian like fashion.

'We certainly are,' replied Tristan. More often than not, it was Charlie and Tristan fighting it out at the finish.

'Well, I'll have to see what I can do about that,' continued Derek. His tone was affable enough, but his smile didn't quite meet his eyes.

Both men nodded at the implied challenge.

'Be our guest,' Charlie replied, stiffly. 'May the best jockey win.'

The afternoon went well for Charlie. Clair de Lune, the black gelding showed some improvement in form to come in fourth, albeit in poor company, after much encouragement from Charlie and Fringe Benefits came in third behind Tristan's mount. The new travelling head lad, Mick Richards was a dark haired chap who was forever bustling about, cleaning a bucket, filling a hay net, plaiting the horses' manes but took time out to shake Charlie's hand enthusiastically. There was also a new stable lad, who had been employed along with Mick called Trevor Marshall, who Mick clearly knew well. Both were clearly very efficient and experienced and seemed to have been appointed together, so Charlie was a little surprised that Miles hadn't mentioned this before.

Charlie noted with satisfaction that Derek's two rides for small trainer, Len Foster, had run down the field. He saw both Len, Derek and Mick chatting together, and it appeared that Derek knew Mick well from the length of their discussion. Still, the racing community was quite small. Perhaps, both had worked in the Epsom area? He couldn't resist grinning cheerily at Derek, but his smile was met by a slight grimace back. Charlie had been pleased to get placed with Clair de Lune, even though it felt like he had almost done all the work himself, so vigorous was his riding at the finish. Clair de Lune was a mediocre horse, but he felt encouraged at what he might achieve with a better mount.

Charlie weighed in and prepared for his next rides for Laura Palmer. Laura was, he guessed, in her early thirties, had long dark hair and the slightly ruddy complexion of a woman used to the great outdoors. She had moved into her small yard only about a year ago and was slowly but surely making substantial progress. She was attractive in an unconventional, wholesome way and Charlie respected her. She was a natural horsewoman and Charlie knew it was only a matter of time before she made her mark on the sport.

Laura beamed at Charlie as he joined the owners in the parade ring. Baltic Bay's owners were a middle aged, pleasant couple who were thrilled to be there. Baltic Bay was a smallish bay horse who looked very well and was immaculately turned out.

'He's been working well at home but it's only his third race over hurdles, so be gentle with him, won't you?' Laura beamed, flushing as she realised how that sounded. 'I mean, he's still only learning so that's the priority really.'

Charlie nodded getting the subtext which was, 'don't push him too hard unless he was in a winning position.' Charlie respected the fact that Laura was so considerate with her horses. Tristan had a ride in this race, but Derek didn't so Charlie relaxed, feeling that he didn't have to prove anything to Tristan. Baltic Bay started out well, but he decided to keep him towards the back of the pack and out of danger for the first circuit and assess how he was going from there. The horse had a good jump and in common with all Laura's horses had been very well schooled which was an added bonus. As they came into the final circuit, Charlie found his bay mount was still full of running and he started to press ahead always taking account the feel of the horse. He was tracking Tristan, riding the promising In the Pink who was now owned by Premiership footballer, Tyler Dalton. Charlie allowed Baltic Bay his head and was delighted to finish third, In the Pink winning by several lengths. The press interest was huge as Tyler's star was rising and he had now been picked for the England squad and as Charlie went into the winner's enclosure, the flashlights were going off everywhere. When Laura's final horse, Have A Go Henry came in a creditable fifth, again much to Laura's delight, he felt he'd had a wonderful day and was feeling extremely pleased with himself. Laura hugged him, her face flushed with happiness.

As he showered, gossiped with Tristan and made his way to his car, he noticed Derek Jones, this time chatting to Miles' other new member of staff, Trevor Marshall. As he reversed his sporty Golf out, he couldn't resist a cheeky wave at Derek, who saw him and turned away. Charlie laughed. It served him right for his earlier remarks. Both he and Tristan had had an excellent day and clearly Derek hadn't, so Charlie felt justified in his actions. They had both put Derek Jones in his place and Charlie couldn't help but allow himself a moment's satisfaction. They were still the gentlemen to beat, as Derek had put it.

At home, his answerphone light was blinking, and he found he had two messages, one from Caroline Regan inviting him to her granddaughter's birthday party and another from his mother asking for him to ring. His mother's quiet, almost depressed voice caused his good mood to deflate in an instant. He flicked through his diary to double check the date. Of course, it was the anniversary of his sister, Helena's accident. Although it was about eight years ago now, Charlie was instantly transported back to that day and the full horror hit him straight between the eyes once again. His parents had separated sometime afterwards, as both struggled with the pain of losing a child and began to drift apart. Rather than ruminate on what might have been, he decided to join a couple of lads in the local. He would ring his mother later. His parents blamed each other following Helena's death and the house had become something of a no man's land between them. But Charlie didn't blame them at all, because he blamed himself. Guilt about Helena and Gina gnawed away at him. It was always like this around the anniversary, but today he had almost forgotten about the weight he had carried around since that dreadful day. His earlier optimism seemed to mock him as he realised he would never be free of the heavy burden of guilt. Now he felt himself staggering under its weight, once more. He knew with dreadful certainty that the vivid, disturbing nightmares would start again.

Chapter 6

'So, how have you been? Did you manage to use the diary we spoke about last week?'

Simon nodded and pulled out the scrunched up booklet Tara had printed for him and tried to flatten it.

Tara eyed the paper dubiously. At least it looked like it had been used, but when she looked again there were what looked like beer stains and something resembling baked bean juice splashed on the front. Her heart sank when he flicked through it and she realised that it hadn't been written in at all.

Simon Norton aged thirty four, was a well dressed young man who worked in sales. He had sought help for his problem gambling following his wife threatening to leave him if he didn't address his habit. So far, he had gambled several months of mortgage repayments away and narrowly avoided repossession of his home by a referral to Citizen's Advice. The final straw had come when he had gambled away the holiday money for their trip of a lifetime to America on a sure thing at Haydock Park. Tara wasn't convinced that he had yet been completely honest about the debt he was in and his marriage was still in an extremely fragile state. Tara had been assigned to undertake Cognitive Behavioural Therapy with Simon and this was their third session. Cognitive Behavioural Therapy was widely used by psychologists and broadly uses the links between thoughts and behaviour to change entrenched problems. Many people's thoughts or 'self talk' is irrational and the therapy seeks to help show this. Research showed it has been effective with people with gambling problems, hence Tara's decision to use it with Simon.

Simon had great difficulty sitting still and tension seeped out of his body, as he shuffled uncomfortably in his seat, hands cupping the back of his head.

'Well, I sort of started off OK for a couple of days, then I convinced myself to buy a couple of scratch cards and then had a small bet on the two o' clock at Wetherby.' Simon flushed, then gave Tara a challenging look, as if daring her to reprimand him.

'OK. Progress is at your own pace, so let's unpick how you felt, say for example before you decided to buy the scratch cards?'

Again, Simon's wriggling intensified. 'Sort of bored, I suppose...'

'What were you doing at the time?'

'Oh,' Simon screwed up his face as he tried to remember. 'It was Wednesday, I'd had a shit day at work, the boss was moaning about our sale figures, the missus was giving me grief as soon as I got in about bailiffs or summat, the kids were arguing...' Tara paused waiting for him to continue. Simon sighed as he struggled to articulate his thoughts. 'Then, I just kept thinking about winning, how proud the missus would be, the kids and that. There's lots of people who have won big prizes, five grand, ten even, a hundred so I thought, why not me?' He looked at Tara imploringly.

'What happened then?'

Simon ran his hands through his thick blond hair. 'Me and Lisa, well she would only stay with me if she had control of the money, all the credit cards. She gives me twenty quid at a time for lunches, petrol and stuff. So, I saved a couple of quid and went off to the newsagents on the corner...'

'OK. So how did you think and feel just before that point?'

Simon scratched his nose. 'How do you think? Crap, I work all the hours God sends and Lisa take all me money. I felt less of a man, I suppose, pissed off...'

'How did you feel when you were in the newsagents?'

Simon frowned with the effort of thinking back. 'Sort of angry, I'll show her, she'll change her tune as soon as I win. And then excited, I really had a good feeling, you know? This time, I'm gonna do it. I really thought I would win. Someone's got to win these things, so why shouldn't it be me?'

Tara jotted down this flawed logic. Why shouldn't it be him but equally why should it be him when the odds were absolutely vast? Tara studied him, willing him to make the link between his thoughts, feelings and then actions which was the essence of CBT.

Simon screwed up his face whilst he concentrated.

'So, can you think back to what we talked about last week about how your thoughts affect your feelings and then your behaviour?'

Realisation appeared to dawn. 'Oh. Like how thinking everything was crap, made me feel angry and annoyed… Oh yeah. So, to feel better I went straight out and had the bloody bet, didn't I?'

Tara nodded. 'So, if you think back to what we said last week, we have to look at those thought patterns and change those first.'

Simon blinked, and he leant forward in his chair. 'Oh, right. Easy, innit?'

Tara felt that the penny was starting to drop and began to think she had made some progress. At least Simon was starting to consider how his thoughts, emotions and behaviour were interlinked, which was a start. But there was a long way to go. She smiled.

'If we try to do the same with your other bet. It was on horse racing, wasn't it?'

Simon nodded. 'Only, that was different because it was a proper tip from a mate, see. It took real skill for them to look at the odds, previous races, distances, which stables are in form, you see, to come up with it. There are lots of factors. It's really complicated, and it takes a great deal of knowledge to be a tipster.'

Tara realised that it was going to require more time to unravel Simon's beliefs about betting tips, which he still saw as less risky and based on inside information or skilful interpretation of the facts. At least that gave her something to work on. Simon's twitching was even more severe, so she guessed that this bet was considerably larger. He was making her feel exhausted just watching him. She took a deep breath.

'Well, let's go through the same process about how you were thinking and feeling before that bet then, shall we, in as much detail as you can?'

It was ironic, Tara thought, that when things were looking up in her professional life and she felt her placement was coming together, matters in her personal life had taken a complete nosedive. She picked at her sandwich whilst she flicked through her emails in the office and wondered what on earth to do about Callum. It was now Monday and she had heard sight nor sound of him since Saturday. She had texted him a couple of times, but he had not responded, and she felt completely and utterly undecided about what to do next. Various scenarios swirled through her head, but mostly she just felt confused and worried. She was finding it increasingly difficult to concentrate on anything and the more she stewed over likely scenarios, the worse she began to feel. Change your thoughts, she told herself crossly, thinking back to her CBT training. A fine psychologist she was going to make if she couldn't even use the techniques on herself, what hope did she have of encouraging other people to do it? Eventually, she hummed and hawed and as the office was quiet, she finished writing up her case notes and decided to ring his mobile. After several seconds someone answered. She could hear the sound of breathing at the other end of the line.

'Hi, Callum. Thank goodness, is everything OK?'

There was a brief pause and what sounded like heavy breathing. She heard a woman in the background say, 'Pass the phone to daddy, Alfie. Come on there's a good boy.' It was a lovely cultured voice. Relaxed, happy and amused. Anna.

'I'm Alfie, who are you?' said a child's voice, in a singsong manner. She could hear further heavy breathing and Callum chatting to Anna in the background. It sounded amiable and normal.

'Come on Alfie, pass me the 'phone.'

It was Callum. There was a rushing sound and a child's giggle, and the sound of thundering feet. Stunned, Tara rang off in confusion, her heart pounding. The family scene sounded nice, normal and perfectly happy. Not at all like they were in hospital, dealing with a sick child, contemplating terrible things. Mobile phones weren't even allowed in hospitals, were they? The exchange had sounded so normal, ordinary and definitely not what she had been expecting. She felt as though she had glimpsed a private family moment she had no business intruding into. It was the intimacy she was shocked by. She didn't know exactly what an ill child sounded like, but Alfie hadn't sounded ill. He sounded in extremely good health and ill children certainly didn't answer their parents' mobiles and run off with them, did they? The implication of this snapshot of family life was all too clear.

Chapter 7

Charlie led the chestnut gelding, bedecked with a red bow on his head collar, to the driveway and stood in front of the expectant guests. Outside Bramble Hall, all the party had assembled dutifully donning their coats over their party finery. Even to Charlie's untutored eyes, there were several well known actors and Hollywood 'A' listers present and the whole scene set in front of the exquisite, brick Georgian house seemed ridiculously decadent. Charlie murmured to the horse, Rose Gold, in order to keep him calm and hoped that the ridiculous ribbon that Caroline had insisted he wear tied to his headcollar didn't blow off and cause him to bolt.

'Steady boy. It's alright.' Charlie scanned the crowd.
Caroline had donned a long cream mac and was still holding a flute of champagne. She was arm in arm with a slight, beautiful dark haired girl, he presumed was Tara.

'Happy birthday, darling. This is your present from me, Rose Gold...' There was an uncertain pause and then a delighted ripple of applause.

'Marvellous, what a splendid idea,' shouted someone.

'Well, she's bloody well surpassed herself this time,' muttered another. Miles stood to one side and then moved forward to greet the girl. She was wearing a lavender coloured slip dress, no coat and very high nude heels. She was very slender and delicate looking. She just gazed at Rose Gold and then Charlie in astonishment. Miles stepped forward.

'Hmm. Hello, I'm Miles Jamieson and I'm going to be training Rose Gold and this is my stable jockey, Charlie Durrant. Charlie this is Tara Regan.' Miles beamed.

Charlie looked at the delicate face and stuck out his hand. Tara's dark eyes appraised him. She shook his hand, her gaze flickering over the horse, uncertainly.

Caroline studied Tara's face anxiously. 'You see it's all arranged, Tara. I will pay the training fees and I just want you to go along to the races and have some fun, darling. And,' she stretched out her free hand to Charlie's, 'I've asked this gorgeous man to spend some time with you to negotiate the whole racehorse owner thing.'

Charlie winced at the description of him as 'gorgeous', but then decided he would quite like Tara to think that about him, as her dark eyes flickered over him.

Tara patted the horse and suddenly looked tearful. She turned to her grandmother, her eyes glistening.

'Thank you, granny. He is absolutely divine. It's the nicest present anyone has ever bought me.' There were tears, hugs and collective sighs from the crowd who were itching to go back inside into the warmth of Bramble Hall. A distinguished looking man, Charlie recognised as Lawrence Prendergast, Caroline's son- in-law came forward and shook Miles' hand warmly. He nodded briefly to Charlie.

'Of course, Lawrence has been so clever in buying Rosie,' continued Caroline, absently patting Rose Gold's muzzle.

'He's extremely well bred,' Lawrence continued, launching into one of his monologues about dams, sires and breeding lines. Charlie felt in his pocket for a polo mint and fed it to Rose Gold. The horse munched it and then nudged Charlie clearly wanting another one. Charlie patted his head as he munched. He lifted his forelock, the long piece of mane that grew between his ears, and noticed he had two small circular whorls, so would pass the Jack Farnham double whorl test like Zorba the Greek. Hopefully, that would mean he would turn out to be a good one. He found he really hoped for Tara's sake that Jack was right.

'Now, let's go back in and enjoy the party,' continued Caroline, in a voice that brooked no opposition. 'And you two must come back when you've sorted out dear Rosie,' she continued, looking at Charlie and Miles. Charlie had been about to slope off, but something about Tara's rather forlorn expression prevented him. She looked a little lost somehow. Miles leapt at the opportunity to join the party and had no intention of letting Charlie disappear.

'We'll just hand over Rose Gold to the lad to take him back to the stables and then we're all yours, aren't we Charlie?'

Caroline smiled and said in her best Bond girl tones. 'Splendid, darlings. I want you to meet everyone.'

About fifteen minutes later when Rose Gold was returned to the lorry, where Mick Richards was waiting to drive him back to Thornley House, Charlie and Miles were ushered into Caroline's impressive living room and handed champagne and hors d'oeuvres, served by smart waiters. A string quartet played soothing classical music. Charlie scanned the room. By the huge stone fireplace there was Nils Sorensen, the Hollywood director surrounded by lithe young men and women, who were hanging on his every word. Caroline was lounging on a chaise longue holding court, whilst Tara stood with several young women who were looking round in amazement at the guests. A young man with astonishing cheekbones and the same dark eyes as Tara was telling jokes to several lads. These seemed to be outrageously funny if the raucous laughter was anything to go by. In another corner, stood a young man, who even Charlie recognised as the last Doctor Who, and there were several familiar looking people who Charlie realised were well known actors. There was also another group of adults of varying ages who Charlie reckoned by their slightly uneasy expressions, were relatives who, like him, were feeling a little overawed by the guest list. From this group, a fair haired, middle aged man dressed in a pinstriped suit came to greet them followed by a smiley woman.

'Hello there. Thank you so much for coming. I'm Jack Regan, Caroline's son and Tara's father and this is my wife, Kate.' The man looked from Miles to Charlie and back again. He was very like Caroline. 'It's rather an extravagant present my mother had bought for Tara. She does rather spoil her, but Ma has said you are both going to help Tara with Rose Gold. I don't think Tara knows the first thing about racing and all the etiquette and what not.'

'Yes, yes that's right. Well, it's quite straightforward really. You must come down to Thornley House to see the facilities. We are a very progressive yard, I like to think.' Miles started to talk about training regimes and swimming pools whilst Tara's mother struck up a conversation with Charlie.

'So, you're the jockey Caroline has told us so much about? Well, it's lovely to meet you and if you can help Tara get to grips with owning Rose Gold, then we would be so grateful.' She smiled and gave her daughter a brief, worried glance. 'Tara is rather a serious and career minded and she's training to be a psychologist. She's been very stressed of late, so I think Caroline just wanted her to have some fun. She's studying for a doctorate, you see.'

Charlie nodded. He didn't really see but glanced at Tara again. Studying for a doctorate didn't sound particularly fun, he had to admit. She was clearly not the spoilt, rather self centred young woman he had assumed she would be. He had no idea what psychologists did apart for probably analyse troubled people, but it sounded worthy and rather impressive.

'Of course, I'll help all I can. I can explain about all the races and so on. Rose Gold is an excellent choice.' Charlie was glad he had looked up Rose Gold's breeding and racing history in preparation for his role as racing advisor. 'He's a four year old gelding who showed a bit of form on the flat and has had one race as a four year old over hurdles but showed promise in terms of stamina and jumping ability. Miles will supervise his schooling and general fitness and then we'll see how we go.'

Kate nodded but her eyes continually flickered towards Tara, which betrayed a combination of pride and concern, he noticed. He wondered why she should be so worried about her.

Kate smiled at him and patted his arm. 'That would be wonderful. Tara always wanted to learn to ride but somehow ballet and piano lessons took over, as they do. Perhaps, you could teach her? Would Rose Gold be suitable to learn on?'

Charlie frowned, wondering if Kate had got the wrong end of the stick. Why if Tara wanted to learn to ride, hadn't Caroline bought her a ladies' hack instead of a racehorse? He tried to think of a diplomatic way to say this.

'Probably not. Thoroughbreds can be rather flighty and bred for speed but I'm sure Miles could find a school master type for her to learn on, if she really wants to learn.'

Kate looked at him hopefully.

Miles overheard. He nodded at something Jack said and then glanced at Charlie.

'I'm sure I can think of something. We still have an old chaser at home, Lennie, who is as safe as houses. She could learn on him. You'll be fine to teach her, won't you?' Miles' eyes were burning into him and he felt Miles' elbow nudging into his side. Charlie looked at Tara who had suddenly come to join their group. She had an expectant expression and he didn't have the heart to refuse her.

'Yes, I'm sure we can arrange something.'

Miles looked on. 'And Jack was just suggesting that they come around to the yard tomorrow, so they can see Rose Gold work out. You will be able to ride him, won't you? It would be so good to get a professional jockey's view of his capabilities rather than one of work riders...' Miles explained. 'Charlie will be able to tell in an instant what's what.'

Suddenly, Caroline and Tara and everyone else seemed to be within earshot, eagerly awaiting Charlie's response. He had been going to see his mother tomorrow but decided that the visit would have to be delayed. He felt Tara's solemn gaze upon him and made up his mind.

'Sure, that's no problem at all,' he lied.

Caroline beamed. 'You see I told you he was wonderful,' she purred. Charlie smiled uncertainly, wondering what exactly what he was getting himself into.

The following morning, Charlie rode Rose Gold up to the gallops accompanied by a couple of other horses, one of whom was Caroline's horse Indian Ocean whilst Tara, Caroline, Jack and Kate followed behind in Miles' Land Rover. It was a chilly but bright morning. Charlie felt his spirits rise as he breathed in the fresh air. He and Miles had left the party fairly early, after Miles having gained several potential new owners, impressed with the fact that he was the son of Nathaniel Jamieson. No doubt, they thought he had inherited his father's horsemanship and together with his 'progressive' methods, hoped great success would follow. These were, in Miles' view, his unique selling points as a trainer and he had had high hopes that some of the interest that was shown by the rather grand guests last night, might well translate into new owners. Even Dr Who, or the actor who played him had declared an interest in owning a racehorse, but not so much that he was in attendance this morning, Charlie noted rather sourly. Caroline, Miles told him, had been delighted with Charlie offering to teach her granddaughter to ride and had been extolling his virtues all night. It seemed a little churlish to explain that that was not quite how Charlie remembered it.

The Land Rover pulled up at a good vantage point on the gallops and the party stiffly climbed out the vehicle. Caroline was looking a little worse for wear, Charlie noticed whilst Tara looked surprisingly fresh in her jeans and warm jacket, her hair scooped up into a messy ponytail affair. Her parents looked on with interest.

'Right, just canter them round for a few furlongs then try some of the hurdles,' suggested Miles.

Charlie fastened the strap on his helmet, lowered his goggles and urged Rose Gold into a trot, then a canter. The wind rushed by as Rose Gold obligingly sped on following Indian Ocean and Fringe Benefits. Charlie made encouraging noises with his tongue to urge him into a gallop. The chestnut was obliging enough but seemed rather one paced and began to lag behind his training mates. Charlie urged him on a little with his legs and heels but there was precious little acceleration. Perhaps, he wasn't fit, had virus or just was plain slow? Either way, he did not show any of the promise his rather superior parentage had promised. So much for the double whorl test.

Over the training jumps, he did however show some scope and ability to jump neatly and safely which was something. As Charlie undid his helmet strap, he tried to think of non committal comments that would offer hope yet not actively mislead the expectant group which waited for him to give his verdict. Of course, it was still early days and Charlie wasn't exactly sure of the horse's training regime recently. Perhaps, he had been turned away and not been worked since the previous owners had decided to sell him? In that case, that might explain his mediocre form. Miles was looking at him carefully, he noticed.

'So, what did you think of Rosie?' asked Caroline. Tara was gazing at him.

'Well, he shows promise,' continued Charlie carefully. 'He is a little unfit, but his jumping is very good.' Perhaps, he would make a better show jumper, he almost added. Miles eyed him uneasily. There was a collective sigh as the group patted Rose Gold and made appreciative remarks.

'Of course, we don't know how much work he has done recently,' continued Miles. 'But I'm sure with the swimming sessions, solarium and a tailor made training plan, he will really improve.'

Caroline had regained some of her joie de vivre, Charlie noticed. But perhaps this was also to do with her swigging liberally from a large hip flask. Hair of the dog, he presumed.

'Splendid, darlings. Indy looks very well too. Now, when is Rosie going to be running?'

'Quite soon,' answered Miles, to Charlie's surprise. 'In fact, I think he has been entered in some races from his last yard. One is next week, if my memory serves me correctly. 'I think he will be ready, then.'

Caroline gasped, and Tara grinned, almost hopping with excitement.

Charlie tried to compose his face into a neutral expression to hide his surprise. Surely, it was far too early to consider racing him? What the hell was going on?

Chapter 8

Tara heard her 'phone buzz and quickly glanced at it. It was yet another message from Callum. She had been bombarded with them since her call to him a few days ago. She sighed. Again, he texted to say he was keen to meet and explain himself. She deleted it as she had done all the rest. Since that time, she had alternated between thinking there was a reasonable explanation for the cosy exchanges she had overheard and being furious for what could also be interpreted as plain deceit. At some point she knew it would be reasonable to allow Callum the opportunity to explain himself, but she couldn't face it right now. Whatever the explanation, she had come to realise that it was she who couldn't cope with the fact that he had a child. A child who sounded sweet and lovely and an entire shared history with Anna that couldn't be undone. She hated the way it made her feel. She had already decided that whatever Callum's explanation, because he was bound to come around or force her to listen at some point, she would tell him that the relationship was over.

Until now she had indulged in a strange sort of fantasy that Anna had somehow forced Callum to marry her against his will and that the whole thing had been a huge mistake. Indeed, Callum had sort of fuelled this by explaining that Anna's father was a senior Partner in the law firm he worked for. The firm had taken him on against the odds. So, he sort of owed her father something, so much so that he felt obliged to marry his daughter. But she realised just from that tiny glimpse into their lives and after listening to the snatches of conversations she had overheard, that it wasn't at all like that. She sensed that Callum wasn't ready to end his relationship and that to avoid herself future pain, she should just bow out gracefully and leave them to sort things out. She would simply excise these last six months from her life and carry on as though it had never happened. Of course, she expected to change her mind several times a day about this, but in calmer more lucid moments, this was her preferred course of action for now at least. There was always the possibility that her logic would melt away when confronted by the physical presence of Callum and his considerable charisma, but this was what she knew she *ought* to do. And she had the added advantage of being able to take the moral high ground and return a married man back to his wife and child, which was an added, though, undeniably painful bonus.

Gabriella and Emily had been a sounding board for Tara too. But both had different opinions. They were sat in their shared kitchen sipping tea.

'Well, I think you should just meet Callum and at least hear what he has to say. Supposing Alfie was ill but was then given the all clear and they were just spending time together in the fall out?' Emily suggested. She was a fellow clinical psychologist trainee and a great believer in talking therapies which she felt could solve everything. 'If you two just talk it through, I'm sure it will all be resolved.'

Gabriella tossed her blonde curls in annoyance. She worked in finance and had a rather more prosaic view of life.

'No, no, no,' she exclaimed emphatically. 'Just don't waste your time with him. There's plenty more fish in the sea. There was so much talent at your party. All those gorgeous actors, for instance...' Gabriella had been rather entranced by Fraser, Tara's brother and Damien Jones, the Dr Who actor. She had left the party having given her telephone number to Damien and Fraser. She had high hopes of seeing one of them again after flirting first with Damien and then with Fraser after Damien had left.

'I rather liked the look of the jockey, Charlie wasn't it?' commented Emily. 'I thought jockeys were usually tiny, but he was tall and rather handsome. Lovely eyes.'

Tara found herself being scrutinised by her housemates. If she were honest, she had found the whole party rather awkward. She had sort of slept walked through the whole thing. She had been too confused and upset by thoughts of Callum to really enjoy it. She was delighted by her grandmother's gift of Rose Gold, but rather bemused at the same time. It was one of her Granny's more outrageous gifts and completely impractical. Still, she had found the chestnut gelding rather lovely and Miles and Charlie perfect gentlemen. She wasn't at all sure that she even approved of horse racing, thinking back to her work with gambler Simon Norton. Still, as with many of Caroline's great ideas, she found that if she allowed herself to be swept along then she would become almost as enthusiastic as Caroline. This was probably no exception.

Emily was still studying her, trying to gauge her reaction to what she had said about Charlie.

'So, what did you think about Charlie?'

Tara shrugged. 'Well, he seemed very nice. I hardly spoke to him really. Granny has asked him to advise me on all aspects of racing though.'

Gabriella snorted. 'I think she has other ideas, knowing your grandmother otherwise she would have asked the trainer to advise you. Wouldn't that make more sense?'

Emily nodded. 'Well, the trainer, Miles was OK, but that jockey was really lovely. He had a real twinkle in his eye.'

Tara flushed slightly. The thought that her grandmother might be trying to set her up with Charlie had crossed her mind, as had the realisation that she had also guessed about the true state of Tara's love life. Caroline had an uncanny intuition where Tara was concerned and all those probing questions about the whereabouts of Tara's young man and her awareness of Tara's mood changes and caginess on the subject, had probably led her Granny to draw the right conclusion, that her love interest was married. Not for the first time, she had to admire her grandmother's instincts and ability to see right through her. Well, if her Granny had gone to all the bother of buying her a beautiful racehorse so she could enjoy herself, who was she to look a gift horse in the mouth? Quite literally. She found the more she thought about it, she was looking forward to being a racehorse owner. She would worry about the ethics later, for now she really did need a major distraction, she decided.

Charlie had postponed his visit to his mother in order to ride Rose Gold but had spent the following evening tossing and turning, his old dreams encroaching into his consciousness. He dreamt that his sister was running ahead of him in the meadow they used to play in as children. Helena turned back giggling, desperate for him to catch her up. He ran and ran but she was always ahead of him, just out of reach. Then she disappeared, and dread ebbed over him as he searched frantically for her. But she was nowhere to be seen. He ran this way and that, shouting and calling to no avail. Charlie ran on and came to a fire in the clearing, the smoke choking him. Then there was a spluttering noise as the fire took hold, followed by the rumble of an explosion as a ball of flames leapt into the night sky. He knew Helena was in the flames, as firm hands kept hold of him, he watched transfixed and horrified. Someone was screaming, in desperate pain. Then he realised it was him.

'There's nothing you could have done,' the man whispered. 'It's not your fault.' But Charlie knew he was just being kind. He knew it was his fault for he had not looked after her as he promised his parents he would. As Helena's flesh was engulfed in flames, he knew in his heart that he would carry the responsibility for what had happened to her forever.

He woke with a start and then tried to doze, as endless thoughts chased and chased round his brain. He should have checked on her like he was asked to. She was his little sister who had been so excited to be able to go out with him, as long as he kept an eye on her. That was the only condition laid down by his parents. But he hadn't kept his part of the bargain and now everything was ruined because of him. The shame and guilt churned round and round and the only way he could cope was to avoid the luxury of love. He did not deserve it and he knew it was only a matter of time before those who tried to love him would realise this too.

Charlie's mother looked tired and faded. He kissed her cheek. Barbara Durrant looked older than her fifty two years. The grief of losing a daughter and then a marriage seemed to have squashed the life out of her, somehow. Her shoulder length dark hair was smattered with grey and her blue eyes looked haunted. She was still an attractive woman, though, and was slim and lithe. Charlie thought it was a great pity she hadn't remarried or found someone else since Dad had left.

'How are you?' she scanned his face. 'How's that lovely Gina, you were seeing?'

'Erm… Well, we're not together at the moment.'

Mum nodded. Charlie sat in the living room of his childhood home, a comfortable semi in a leafy area of York. His mother nodded at his comments. She was used to Charlie's girlfriends not staying the course.

'How's the new boss, Miles, working out?'

'He's fine. I miss Nathaniel and he doesn't come down to the yard much these days. But Miles uses very progressive training methods so I'm sure we'll do well this year.'

Barbara smiled. 'Well, I've been watching your progress on the racing channels and you seem to be doing well, love. I watched the race when you won on Indian Ocean, Caroline Regan's horse. She still looks lovely, doesn't she? She was great in those Bond movies.'

Charlie updated her on Caroline and Tara. Barbara was delighted with the glimpse into the glamorous lives of the rich people her son rubbed shoulders with.

'What's she like this Tara, then? Rather spoilt, I should imagine?'

Charlie thought for a minute. 'No, not at all. She seemed rather a decent person, she's training to be a psychologist, actually. That's why Caroline wanted to buy her a racehorse, so she could have a break from her studies.'

Barbara nodded and then edged about uncertainly in her chair.

'There's something I was meaning to say. You know I've been volunteering at the Homeless shelter?' She paused, uncertainly. 'I do enjoy it as you know. Well, they have offered me a permanent job as a support worker. I just wondered what you thought?'

'Great, that's amazing mum. You must take it, you have put so much effort into that place.' Charlie wondered how his mother had turned into the sort of woman who needed her son's permission to work. How had that happened? She was always so strong and efficient when he was a boy. She managed the family home, his father, two small children and a job at the office. She had become depressed and lost her way when Helena died and had been too ill to work. But this was marvellous news.

Barbara smiled. 'Do you think so? It's only part time but I do feel like I'm giving something back. I know that I can offer them something.' Her eyes were shining. She smiled shyly. 'I met him, you know at the shelter...'

Charlie frowned. 'Who? Who do you mean?'

'Jimmie Bird...'

Charlie gulped. Him! The boy that had driven the car that had killed his sister. Who had survived when she hadn't. Amazingly, he had regained consciousness enough to leap out of the car before the flames engulfed it, leaving his sister to die. Rage mingled with disbelief shot through his veins. How could she sit there and say that? It was an insult to his sister's memory. He got up to leave for he was very afraid he might say something he would regret if he didn't. His mother followed him, her face ashen.

'Hear me out, Charlie. Listen, will you? Yes, he survived but his life has been very hard, he's been in and out of prison, got into drugs… I know how you feel, believe me. I used to hate him but he's desperately sorry about what happened, and it's ruined his life too… But we can change that...'

Charlie didn't want to hear anymore.

'How could you even look at him, after everything? Let alone help the bastard?'

He strode to the door, refusing to listen to anything else his mother had to say. But not before he heard her final words.

'Because, I have forgiven him. And you should too. Don't you see it's the only way to move forward and forgive yourself, Charlie…'

Charlie turned on his heel and slammed the door. It seemed he would never, ever be free of what happened that night. It had changed everything.

Chapter 9

Charlie had been asked to ride Rose Gold at the gallops for his last work run before the race at Market Rasen. Charlie rode at the rear of the string, whilst the drizzle seeped into his clothes. They were walking in single file up the track. There were about six of the string, three of which were racing at Market Rasen in the same meeting as Rose Gold. The other horses were Jamaica Inn, a dark bay gelding and Femme Fatale who was a grey mare. Charlie listened to the banter from the lads as he rode.

'Yeah, no one gets a look in or gets to go with their horses to any races these days,' commented Davy, a young stable lad who looked after four horses. He had been appointed by Nathaniel and was used to going to the odd racetrack to look after his charges, accompanied by the Travelling Head Girl, Gina. However, now it seemed that the new appointments Mick Richards and Trevor Marshall always went to the races and the stable lads were not allowed to accompany the horses they cared for anymore.

'Things have really gone downhill since the old guvnor retired,' muttered Neil, another stable lad. 'And I'm not sure about that new vet, Alistair Morgan, either. He's very thick with the new guvnor and is always popping in.'

'Yeah and there's the new cleaner Kim. She's a bit feisty but alright.' Davy gave a low whistle.

Well, that was something, Charlie thought. At least the house should be clean which should help the business, but it was interesting to hear that the lads were being excluded from going to the races. It was usual that the Travelling Head Lad or Girl would go, as that was their role, but other stable lads usually went in turn, to accompany their horses to make sure all their needs were catered for. The lads and lasses usually enjoyed going. It was a perk of the job. Still, no doubt this was another of Miles' progressive ideas.

'And Will and Mick don't really hit it off. They were arguing the other day 'bout summat. Will spoke to Miles, but he weren't interested,' continued Neil.

Charlie wondered what Will, The Head Lad and Mick were arguing about but decided it could be anything. Probably different work practices, or something. Still, it wasn't good if the yard was divided like this. It was amazing what you could pick up if you just listened, Charlie realised. He wondered whether he ought to have a word with Miles about it. Usually, he would have been involved in these discussions, but he felt tired and rather low since the argument with his mother. The initial burst of fury had given way to an overwhelming sadness which threatened to engulf him. He shook his head as if trying to dispel his thoughts.

'Hey, you're quiet,' remarked Davy.

'Bet you're still getting over Caroline's party,' suggested Neil, winking at Davy. 'Heard the champagne was flowing and the women were gorgeous. I bet you enjoyed yourself Charlie, boy. Are you still hung over?'

Charlie grinned back. If only it was that simple. 'Something like that...' In the distance he saw Miles' silver Land Rover approaching and tried to concentrate on the job in hand. Miles was not alone. His father Nat sat in the passenger seat. The lads looked on in surprise. Nat hadn't been very visible for a few weeks due to having a bad chest cold. He looked better today and grinned at the assembled ride.

Miles wound his window down, his breath visible in the cold and ran his fingers through his floppy hair.

'Right, let's start with three circuits. Charlie, I want you to really push Rose Gold after the first circuit and report back to me in great detail about how he feels. See if you can match Clair de Lune's pace.'

Nat leapt out of the vehicle. 'Come on then, chop, chop, lads. I'm losing the will to live here,' he quipped. As Charlie adjusted Rose Gold's girth and his goggles, he looked up to see Miles still in the Land Rover and Nat standing on the side of the gallops, studying each horse carefully. It sort of reflected their training style, he thought. Nat was much more involved and out amongst the horses and staff, whereas Miles was so much more remote. He knew which style he preferred.

Charlie set off on Rose Gold tracking the black horse, Clair de Lune as he urged his horse forward. He kept a steady pace. The gallops were five furlongs long, an all weather track which bordered Taylor's Copse, a small area of dense trees. Charlie felt his spirits lifting as the familiar rhythm of the horse's motion took over and the cold air rushed past him. As they came into the third circuit Rose Gold seemed to tire and started to fall back, the marker of Clair de Lune's black hind quarters becoming more and more distant. Charlie urged him on, but the horse clearly had nothing more to give. Rose Gold had given a similar performance to previously and Charlie was beginning to feel that his initial assessment of a one paced, very mediocre animal was in fact depressingly accurate. As he pulled Rose Gold up, he looked back over the horse's ribs. He was breathing reasonably heavily, but there was limited sweat, so it didn't seem to be an obvious fitness issue and as far as he could tell there was no evidence of lameness.

He rode back to where Miles and Nat were waiting.

Nat grinned at Charlie and patted Rose Gold before running his hands over his legs.

'This is the Caroline Regan's granddaughter's horse, is it?' he asked in disbelief. 'Bought off Prendergast, wasn't he? What's your assessment?'

Charlie looked into Nat's shrewd blue eyes. How didn't come down to the yard nearly enough these days.

'He seems fit, no lameness. He jumps well, but considering his staying pedigree and previous form, which I'm told was promising, he's not shown much so far.'

Miles called from the Land Rover, frowning. 'Think I'll get the vet Alistair Morgan to have a quick look at him.'

Nat patted the horse, felt for his pulse near his jaw, where the mandibular artery runs. He winked up at Charlie.

'Could be settling in problem or it could be that Prendergast has got carried away by breeding lines and he isn't going to live up to his promise. I shouldn't imagine he was cheap. Best check with his lad, see if he seems settled and if he's eating up. I'm not sure about the race on Saturday, mind...'

Charlie nodded. It felt great to have Nat back and to have his expert horsemanship to draw upon. He glanced at Miles who was already on his mobile to Alistair, no doubt. Miles would definitely want him to run given he had already told Caroline and Tara about it. He wondered if Miles would take Nat's advice and decided that he would probably be more swayed by the consultation with the new vet.

As predicted, Miles dropped his father off home and was in discussions with Alistair Morgan in the house for several hours. Alistair was a very young, bookish looking man with thick glasses and a diffident manner. He supervised Rose Gold swimming in the horse pool and then placed lots of monitors on him, took a blood sample and felt his legs.

'Well, there's no obvious lameness and his heart seems absolutely fine,' he commented. 'I've taken a blood test, so we'll see if there's any sign of a virus and if not, he'll be fine to run.' He glanced at Charlie and then Miles. 'I just need to speak to you about those samples we were talking about.' It was clear that he did not want to speak in front of Charlie. Alistair and Miles were often talking together and disappearing into the stable next to the swimming pool which had been turned into a storage room. It now contained locked cabinets which only Miles and Alistair had access to. Briefly, Charlie wondered what was in them, then decided it was probably standard veterinary equipment. He left them to it and wandered off to talk to the Head Lad, Will Mellor. Will was barking orders and sorting out the feeds for evening stables.

'So, how are things?' Charlie asked.

Will paused. 'The missus is still being difficult, but that's nothing new. I've just got to get on with it, I suppose.'

Charlie nodded sympathetically. 'How about the boys, is the contact sorted out yet?'

Will grimaced. 'No, not really. She says they don't want to see me at the moment.' Will looked absolutely desolate for a minute. Charlie remembered the boys as really sweet kids who were keen on coming into the yard. Will appeared to dote on them. He remembered him lifting them aloft, so they could pat the horses. It was all so sad. He tried and failed to think of something sensible to say in response.

Will half smiled. 'Well, what can you do? I could see a solicitor but fat lot of good it will do. Anyway. Not sure about all these changes here either, Charlie. I'm not sure at all,' he continued darkly. 'What with all the new staff and the new guvnor wi' all the new fangled ideas in the world, but no bloody horse sense, I'm not sure where it will all end... And with that Mick and Trevor running the show and not letting the lads go to the races, I ask you? It's almost as if...'

Charlie nodded. Will seemed about to say something further, but then thought better of it. Charlie was determined to be upbeat and he had no intention of adding his concerns about the yard into the mix. Yards had a culture of their own and it was possible that things would settle down. Change was inevitable, he thought, but not everyone adapted that well and they had all worked for Nat for several years. It was possible they were just struggling with a new guvnor. He decided to frame a positive response, with touch of flattery thrown in.

'Well, Miles loves his technology and he had a good heart. Just give him a while to settle in. He has a hard act to follow trying to live up to father's standards. And besides, he needs a great Head Lad. We need you, so don't you dare bloody well leave.'

Will grinned showing his gappy teeth. He settled his cap back on his curls.

'Maybe you're right. P'haps, I'll give it a bit longer. Probably owe the old guvnor that much, anyway.'

Charlie patted the older man's arm, pleased. They were all very loyal to Nat, but what would happen when that loyalty ran out?

Miles invited Charlie in later. The house looked sparklingly clean, which was something. Miles noticed Charlie taking this in.

'Yes, I took your advice and got a cleaner in. Her name is Kim, she came highly recommended by Lawrence. She's rather stern but very efficient and can help with the books too, so I'm killing two birds with one stone.'

Charlie nodded, thinking that Lawrence had made a great many recommendations lately and Miles had lapped them all up.

'And the other news is that Rose Gold's results have come through, Alistair pulled some strings to get them analysed quickly and the good news is that he's absolutely fine. Fighting fit in fact. So, he will be racing along with the others on Saturday.'

Charlie took this in. He was struggling not to draw the rather obvious conclusion that if Rose Gold wasn't ill then he must simply be very slow. Surely, Lawrence must have known this and why would he then saddle his niece with such an animal?

'So, if he's not ill then he's just one paced and will run down the field, then?' Charlie couldn't resist adding.

Miles looked at him in surprise. 'Well, I wouldn't quite put it like that, Charlie. There's always room for improvement and with the progressive methods we have here I'm sure he will be just fine.'

Charlie grunted and restrained himself from saying that all the progressive methods in the world couldn't improve a horse with such limited ability as Rose Gold appeared to have.

'Oh, and by the way, Caroline wants you to meet up with Tara before Saturday and just run through the process beforehand with her.'

Charlie shrugged. 'Well, it's quite straightforward really. Can't you do it?'

Miles beamed. 'Listen, when Caroline Regan asks you to do something then you just do it. She is rich and hugely influential. And she has expressly asked for you. Anyway, she could really help us all, a word here and there from Caroline and who knows who else might want to get into racing?' Miles rubbed his hands together almost gleefully. 'And in racing the owners are king.'

Charlie nodded at the truth of this. His misgivings melted away.

'OK. Point taken.'

Chapter 11

Tara was rather surprised to get a call from Charlie Durrant explaining that Rose Gold would be racing at Market Rasen on Saturday and inviting her to meet him to discuss the race day protocol. Surprised but open to the distraction and rather pleased. Then she realised that her grandmother must have asked him to ring her and then felt absurdly deflated. They arranged to meet up in York for a quick drink. After the last couple of weeks, it would be nice to get out and think about someone other than Callum. After ringing her repeatedly, he had decided to write to her explaining the situation. She had read and reread the letter and could practically recite it by heart.

I'm sorry I didn't reply to your text but Alfie was hospitalised overnight and thankfully was given the all clear. A life threatening illness causes you to re-evaluate things. I realise how it must look but I had to be around for a few days to provide some stability for Alfie and support for Anna. However, much as I loved and respected her, I know we can never go back. I want to be with you. The last six months have been wonderful. What can I do to make you understand? Please ring me.
Callum x

However, she still hadn't rung him. The explanation was plausible but the part where he stated he loved and respected Anna told her everything. She felt this should be in the present tense. She had decided rationally and calmly not to ring him, but it didn't mean in less rational moments that she was happy about her decision. She just felt that Callum was still in love with Anna and whilst that was the case, it was pointless to continue their relationship. And throwing a little boy into the mix, well, that was a huge deciding factor. She just couldn't do it. Decisive action now would save her a great deal of pain later, she thought. It was not an easy decision to make and she felt that if she saw Callum she would easily be persuaded otherwise. Her sense of self preservation had kicked in. Leave well alone, she told herself. This is the right thing to do, she knew. But why does it feel so wrong, she asked herself, a million times a day? It was in one of these moods that she set out The Nag's Head public house in York, trying desperately to take her mind off her troubles.

Charlie was already there and deftly ordered her a white wine. The pub was full of character with dark beams, stone flagged flooring and old tables. It was early and there was only a handful of people out. They sat at a table near the huge stone, inglenook fireplace where a fire was blazing. Charlie was wearing a blue shirt which set off his cobalt coloured eyes. Tara took in his dark, good looks. He looked better than she remembered from her party.

'Are you looking forward to the race on Saturday?' he asked.

'Yes absolutely. It's very exciting, actually.' Tara realised it was true. She felt a frisson of expectation and anticipation every time she thought about Rose Gold and his forthcoming race, exactly as her grandmother knew she would.

'So, shall I just run through the main points?'

Tara nodded as Charlie explained that she would be given free entry to the racecourse, badges, access to Owner' and Trainers' facilities and so on. She would be expected to go into the parade ring when the jockeys mounted and meet with Miles and go to the winner's enclosure if they were lucky enough to win or be placed. He went through the weighing in and out process jockeys had to go through and the rudiments of betting. He also explained that as an owner she was free to visit the yard to inquire on her horse's progress. Sunday was usually set aside for this, but she could visit whenever she wanted, provided she rang Miles beforehand. She listened intently.

'So, what about dress codes on race day?' The words were out of her mouth before she's even had time to think about them. Now she sounded fluffy and a bit ridiculous. Damn.

Charlie looked at her with amusement. 'Perhaps, your grandmother could advise you best, but I would say warmth and comfort were paramount, but you should be reasonably smart, of course.'

'So how do you think Rose Gold will run?' Tara asked, trying to keep the expectant air out of her voice.

Charlie paused, and she realised that he was trying to frame his reply carefully. She wondered why.

'Well, I think it will depend. Obviously, he has just moved yards and that can sometimes upset horses and we're not sure of his fitness levels now. So, whilst he shows promise, he is still very much learning about hurdle racing and is a bit green.'

Tara nodded, feeling that of course, it was all much more complicated than she expected. When she thought about it, perhaps it was not at all surprising that Rose Gold might take some time to acclimatise to new surroundings and to hurdle racing. He was an animal after all. It was just that she hadn't really thought about such things.

Charlie was surveying her steadily, as though trying to weigh her up.

'So, what are you studying for again? Only your mum and Caroline said you were rather stressed about your studies...'

Tara grinned. 'I'm studying for a Doctorate in Clinical Psychology at the University of Hull, which means I will become a Clinical Psychologist at the end of the training. I did a Psychology degree at York first and then decided I wanted to further my career and be a professional Psychologist.'

Charlie looked mystified. 'Right. What does a Clinical Psychologist actually do?'

Tara sighed. Sometimes, she wondered that herself, especially when her placement was going badly. 'Well, we're usually employed by the NHS. We can help people with mental health problems, learning disabilities, dementia, people with complex health conditions and children and families. I suppose in a nutshell, we try to apply psychology to a range of human conditions, to improve things really.'

Charlie looked thoughtful. 'Well, it sounds really interesting. I'm just surprised really...'

'Why? I suppose it is a bit of a surprise that Caroline Regan's granddaughter should be involved in something not remotely glamorous.' It was always the same, she realised. People often made a judgement about her without having met her and assumed she would be a wannabe actress or model, but as soon as they did meet her, she wasn't what they expected.

Charlie grinned rather sheepishly and shrugged. 'Well, now that you mention it, I presumed, wrongly as it turned out, that you would be rather spoilt and ...'

'A bit of an airhead?' Tara laughed and so did Charlie. At least he was honest, and it had broken the ice, she supposed. Perhaps, it was time for her to be equally frank.

'Look, Charlie. I know that my grandmother asked you to talk through all this with me and you probably feel obliged to her, but honestly, I don't want to put you to any bother. So now I've got the basics, for which I am eternally grateful, I'll let you get on with your evening.' She got up and started to put on her coat. He was really lovely, but she didn't want him to feel he had to spend the evening with her. He was bound to have something more pressing to do, someone waiting at home for him, a girlfriend or wife. Surely?

Charlie looked at her in surprise. 'Look, I'm enjoying talking to you, honestly. I think you overestimate your grandmother's influence. Even she can't make me do something I don't want to do. And truth to tell, I am at a bit of a loose end myself so if you'd like another drink or even two then, believe me, it would be my pleasure to spend time with you.'

Tara paused and looked at the dark blue eyes fringed with thick lashes. He appeared perfectly genuine, intelligent and good company. But there was something else, an aura of sensitivity or even vulnerability that drew her somehow. This took her completely by surprise. She took off her coat and smiled up at him.

'Well, if you're absolutely sure, I'll have another white wine,' she replied. As she settled down back in her seat and watched Charlie walk to the bar, she realised that she had not thought about Callum once.

The day of the race arrived. Tara settled on a mid length woollen dress, boots and a long coat taking into account Charlie's advice. As Caroline was abroad filming, she opted to go with her parents, Jack and Kate, and housemate Gabriella. As an owner she had four passes and Emily was away that weekend, which thankfully saved arguments between her and Gabriella about who was going to accompany them to the big occasion.

Market Rasen was a lovely, homely course set in Lincolnshire, in the heart of rural England. Tara and her party met up with Miles who explained that Rose Gold was their only runner at Market Rasen as the other two which were entered, Jamaica inn and Femme Fatale had slight injuries, which meant they had been withdrawn on veterinary advice. Charlie had been due to ride them but had picked up another couple of rides for the up and coming trainer, Laura Palmer, instead. As Rose Gold was in the fourth race, they busied themselves studying form and viewing the horses in the parade ring. The horses gleamed and shone, and the jockeys' colours were bright and colourful. It was an intoxicating scene, Tara thought.

'Any tips?' Jack asked Miles.

Miles gave him a slight smile.

'Well, anything Charlie is riding is usually worth a punt or Tristan Davies for that matter. But in terms of trainers, Jeremy Trentham and Adrian Hollinshead, are the ones in form at the moment.'

'What are we to expect from Rose Gold, do you think?' asked Jack.

Tara noticed that Miles showed the same hesitation that she had spotted with Charlie, and general reluctance to commit themselves when specifically asked about Rose Gold and his likely performance.

'Well, he's still learning to be honest and although he is putting in some decent work at home, it's sometimes different on the racecourse. I'm sure he'll put in a workmanlike performance though.' Miles' eyes alighted on a young bespectacled man and he made his excuses. 'Sorry, I have to sort out some paperwork with our vet about the withdrawals. A couple of our horses have trotted up lame at the last minute, so I'll catch you later before the race.' He ran his fingers through his floppy fringe and strode off.

Tara was entranced and exhilarated by the sights and sounds of the racecourse. There were clear areas where only owners and trainers could go, and the course was heaving with interesting looking characters of all ages. There were elderly smart men wearing trilbys and smart older women, horsey looking tweedy types and a handful of young, trendy men and women with furry headbands and beautiful leather boots teamed with expensive tweed jackets. Although a freezing day, the sun was coming out from behind the clouds and bathed the whole scene in sunlight, illuminating the stands and the course. There was a pervasive smell of grass mingled with the scent of expensive perfumes, alcohol, cigar smoke and horse sweat. She heard snatches of conversations about bets, bookies and tips. It was such a different world to what she was used to, but she found it fascinating. She could almost understand Simon Norton and his addiction to gambling as the horses she backed albeit in a small way, looked promising only to fall or be beaten in a blur of colour as they passed the post. The adrenaline rush of anticipating victory was truly thrilling.

She caught sight of Charlie wearing assorted colours, blue hoops and then red with yellow seams. He was placed in one race and was unlucky not to win. The trainer she knew from the race card to be Laura Palmer, looked delighted and hugged him nevertheless, whilst the owners were breathless with excitement. Suddenly it was the fourth race and Tara and her entourage made their way in the parade ring to meet Miles. Rose Gold was being led round by a lad and looked immaculate. He was a chestnut Tara knew, but she thought he looked exactly the colour of a ginger nut biscuit. He was certainly on his toes and needed holding back by his lad. Then the jockeys came out. Charlie was wearing the same colours as he rode in for Caroline, purple and gold hoops which shimmered in the sunshine. He touched his cap as he looked at Tara and her entourage and muttered, 'ma'am' with a broad grin. How quaint, Tara thought.

'Just do your best,' she said, feeling rather embarrassed as she had no clue what to say or do and certainly no advice about how Charlie should ride the race.

'He looks divine,' whispered Gabriella.

'Doesn't he just,' Tara replied. It was only then that she realised that Gabriella was looking at Charlie not Rose Gold. Tara swatted Gabriella's arm, hoping that Charlie hadn't heard her.

'Win or lose, it's an adventure,' replied her mother in measured tones. 'We will still have a drink in the bar afterwards, whatever happens.'

'Yes, yes, you must join me,'said Miles overhearing. He pointed to a large bay horse with a pale faced jockey on board. 'Look that's Rum Cove, the red hot favourite. Rose Gold is way out in the betting at 25-1.' Tara checked her race card and realised that the favourite was being ridden by a jockey called Derek Jones. Blond, thin and almost deathly white, he looked rather puny. She was glad Derek wasn't riding for her.

The horses cantered down to the start and Tara suddenly felt sick with nerves. How on earth did Charlie cope?

Then they were under orders and were off as the tape went up. Her father trained his binoculars on Charlie and Rose Gold whilst Tara squinted trying to see and listened to the crackling commentary. Rose Gold was going well in the middle of the field. They thundered round the first circuit and Rose Gold was still in it and moving slowly up the field. Rum Cove suddenly made his run and was the frontrunner as the group started to break up. Tara could hardly bear to look as Rose Gold started to move away from the field in chase of Rum Cove. There was just one fence to go and Rose Gold was gaining at every stride. He jumped the last fence well, landing just ahead of Rum Cove who appeared to stumble. The crowd began to roar as Charlie began to coax his mount forward. Rum Cove seemed to recover and started to come back, but in a total blur there was an enormous cheer as Rose Gold accelerated and pulled away, winning by about three lengths in the end. Tara hugged her parents, Gabriella and even Miles who looked rather awkward. They had done it! Tara felt as high as a kite. Now she realised what her grandmother had meant. It was an amazing feeling.

Miles beamed at them. 'Come on, let's meet Charlie and go down to the winner's enclosure. He placed his hand in the small of her back and negotiated the steps through the crowd, where a steaming Rose Gold was being led in. There was a huge cheer and Charlie gave a wry smile. Charlie dismounted, and she saw him muttering to Miles urgently. He seemed puzzled, angry even. Miles replied, appearing to be calming him down. Charlie clearly wasn't happy about something. Then, abruptly, he unclipped his helmet and came over to speak to her.

Tara grinned. 'Well done. That was amazing.'

Charlie nodded. 'Yes, I was just saying to Miles, he seemed like different horse today. He didn't quite show that speed on the gallops, but sometimes horses are like that. You can never tell. I'm really delighted we could win for you.'

'Splendid, my dear fellow, well done,' continued her father. 'You must join us later in the bar.'

Charlie grinned and posed for photographs. He was, Tara realised, the ultimate professional. This was his world and he was highly skilled and relaxed within it. Her admiration for him was growing. He was, she realised, something of a pin up boy within the racing world because of his good looks, but he was also very well respected and admired for his horsemanship and riding. He smiled and accepted the congratulations graciously. She wondered fleetingly what he had been speaking to Miles about just after the race. She had the strangest feeling that there was something going on, almost as if Rose Gold's performance had taken him by surprise. Then she dismissed the thought. Their discussion could have been about anything. She linked arms with her father as they made their way to the bar to celebrate. She couldn't wait to tell Caroline. If her current high spirits were anything to go by then her grandmother's choice of birthday present had been absolutely inspired.

Chapter 12

'What? He just hasn't turned up? I don't bloody believe it...' Miles spat out the words in disgust. They had returned from Market Rasen races to find the whole yard in chaos. Apparently, the Head Lad, Will Mellor, had not arrived for work and Neil and Davy and were finishing off by filling hay nets and water buckets and making sure all the horses got their feeds.

'No, he was due in later, as he said he had a meeting or something and he never came in at all...' explained Neil with a shrug. 'It's not like him, even if he's hung over, he's always here...'

Charlie glanced at Miles, wondering if he was aware of the extent of Will's drinking lately. He seemed to be increasingly oblivious to everything. As he had driven back and given Miles a lift, he'd had had the opportunity to discuss his concerns regarding Rose Gold and his rather spectacular form that day. Charlie had been amazed by the change in the horse and not much surprised him these days. Horses usually didn't perform poorly at home and then amazingly well on the racecourse. But Miles had just dismissed the dramatic change in Rose Gold's form by saying that you could never tell with horses and some of them only really 'performed' on the race course, being buoyed up by the atmosphere and the roar of the crowd. It was an atmosphere that was very hard to replicate at home. Training on the gallops just couldn't generate the realism. Charlie had had some experiences of horses like that, but never had known the change to be so marked. Still, Tara and her family were utterly delighted which was something, he supposed.

The horsebox carrying Rose Gold had already returned. He and Miles had been delayed by having a celebratory drink with Tara and her family. Then

Tara's uncle, Lawrence Prendergast had turned up and they had been chatting for a while, but fortunately Trevor and the Travelling Head Lad Mick, had left ahead of them and were back, already pitching in to help.

'I can't believe it,' muttered Miles as he filled yet another water bucket. 'I'll give Will his bloody marching orders if he doesn't have a good explanation, letting us all down like that. And he can kiss goodbye to a reference, too.'

'Steady on.' Charlie thought back to his recent conversation with Will and thought he was sure he would have a good excuse. Something must have happened. 'It's completely out of character, Miles. I mean have you ever known him miss work, ever? Something must have happened.'

Trevor and Miles discussed overtime and further arrangements, so that the yard would be covered if Will was still not back. Charlie fished in his pocket for his mobile and scrolled through to Will's contact details. He rang the number. There was no response, just a pleasant voice asking if he wanted to leave a voicemail. It was no surprise really. Will didn't hold with anything new fangled and still had a battered, vintage Nokia that he forgot to charge up most of the time. Charlie pulled up his collar against the cold. Perhaps, he would pop round to Will's cottage later or swing by The Yew Tree in Walton where he suspected he would find him? Drunk and out of it probably. Perhaps, he had some unwelcome news about the situation with his wife and children? Charlie made up his mind to finish off there and try and find Will. It was the least he could do really, as Will had always played fair with him and spoken up for him when he started out.

Charlie had only had one glass of champagne and had pecked at some food at the racecourse, so he grabbed a banana from home and set off to Will's cottage which was at the other side of the village. He pulled up outside the row of farm cottages, which were lit up by the streetlight, and made his way to the one at the extreme left which he knew belonged to Will. The cottage was in total darkness and although he hammered on the door, he also realised that Will's navy Vauxhall car wasn't there either. Tentatively he tried the door thinking that maybe Will had walked home and left his car at the pub or perhaps he had had a lift home? However, the door was clearly locked. He pulled out his torch from his pocket and made his way round to the back of the house. There was a six foot high fence but he managed to reach over and lift the latch on the rear gate and entered the lawned rear garden. He strode down a couple of steps to the back door. Again, he hammered on the door and when there was no response tried the handle. It was also locked. He shone his torch into the kitchen window, which illuminated a pile of dirty pots in the sink, with more plates stacked up on the kitchen table. There were some children's pictures pinned to the fridge, daubed with the words 'daddy' in huge wonky writing, he noticed with a pang. It must be so incredibly difficult, he realised, when marriages broke up, especially when there were kids involved. One of his mates had described his experience of stilted McDonald's visits with his daughter and the pain of very infrequent contact. Poor Will. Still, the silly old sod would just have to get a grip and get on with it. Charlie intended to tell him that when he found him.

He wondered about checking with the neighbours but decided that a quick visit to The Yew Tree would probably resolve everything. He turned his car round and set off the four miles or so into Walton. The road was narrow and remote and took him over Blackthorn Hill. He picked his way in the slight fog that had descended and changed gear as he rounded a sharp bend almost at the top of the hill. His headlights illuminated a shape to his left which looked vaguely like a car. Perhaps, Will had broken down, but as he approached, he realised it was simply a large sign on some new iron gates to the track on the left that led to Blackthorn Hill Farm. *Danger Keep Out* was daubed in red paint. He knew Blackthorn Hill Farm had once been owned by a permit holder who he used to ride for called Graham Price, but since his death it had fallen into disrepair. It was a shame really. He made himself concentrate on the fog and suddenly as he descended the hill, it completely vanished. He glanced at his watch and sped on. He was sure he would find Will propping up the bar in The Yew Tree.

So confident was he that when he rounded the corner into The Yew Tree car park and realised that Will's car wasn't there, he started to get worried. Where the hell was he? Hadn't Neil mentioned something about him having a meeting or something? Perhaps, there was a family crisis and he hadn't been able to ring into the yard. He parked up and made his way into the main bar.

'Now then Charlie, what'll you have?' asked the barman. A quick exchange revealed that Will hadn't been there all evening. Puzzled, Charlie made his way back to Thornley. A horrible thought occurred to him, that Will might have thought better of giving Miles a bit longer to settle in and had actually upped and left, but again he dismissed that. Will was the epitome of rock solid and reliable and he couldn't see him just leaving. Anyway, he was too much of a horseman to leave the horses without their feeds. None of it made any sense. He made his way home, his head full of Rose Gold's win, Tara's delighted face, the strange improvement in the horse's form and Will's disappearance. Despite his win on Rose Gold something still felt off, wrong, misaligned somehow. He was pleased to win, but his instincts told him something wasn't right. He felt a sense of foreboding as if things were changing and hurtling along at a fast pace in the wrong direction. He went to bed, his head spinning and worry gnawing away at him.

The next day when he was checking on his rides for Wetherby and about to set off, a police car rolled slowly into the yard. Two officers, one in uniform and the other in a suit got out and asked to speak to Miles Jamieson. Charlie looked on his heart sinking. What did they want? It soon became apparent when Miles' ashen face appeared in the doorway of Thornley House. He beckoned Charlie over.

'You'd better hear this,' he murmured as he led into him into the kitchen where the officers were waiting. He could tell by their grave faces that something awful had happened.

The older of the two officers was plain clothed, wore an ill fitting grey suit and had a slight Scottish accent. He introduced himself as DCI Jordan and his uniformed colleague as PC Flintham. PC Flintham looked barely out of school. DCI Jordan looked at Charlie inquiringly.

'I'm the stable jockey, Charlie Durrant. What can we help you with?'

DCI Jordan paused. 'I understand that William Mellor was employed here?' Charlie noticed the past tense and felt sick.

'Yes, he still is employed as the Head Lad. He's been here from my father's day,' continued Miles, a little pompously.

DCI Jordan nodded. 'Well, I'm afraid I have some bad news, Mr Jamieson. Yesterday Mr Mellor's vehicle was found on the road out to Walton, in a remote spot. It appeared that he was travelling at some speed around a blind bend. We're not exactly sure what happened but he seems to have lost control of the car, spun off the road and hit a tree. Seemingly he died instantly.'

Miles gasped in horror. 'Oh my God!'

Charlie felt the room beginning to spin slightly and he clutched the edge of the table. He had travelled that very road in search of Will last night. He knew it well. The road climbed steeply up Blackthorn Hill and had been cut into the hillside. Halfway along there was a blind bend. The road dropped sharply down the hillside on the drive down which is where Will's car must have left the road.

'Can I ask when this happened?'

DCI Jordan sighed. 'I'm afraid we're not exactly sure but he was found at around 11 am yesterday. At least that was then we were informed by a passing motorist. It's a quiet spot, so it would have happened sometime before. There's been some delay because we had to inform his next of kin first.'

A dark haired, pale young woman appeared wearing rubber gloves and holding a bottle of bleach. She looked like a goth with her black hair and piercings. This must be Kim. She looked gravely at them taking in the expression on their faces.

'I'll make some tea,' she said.

The police left after about half an hour promising to come back later in the week to get some statements.

DCI Jordan paused briefly to speak to Charlie before he left, having been given a potted history regarding the state of Will's marriage.

'Yes, we had to break the news to Mrs Mellor yesterday but there was a slight delay in locating her.' Charlie glanced at DCI Jordan's set expression and tried to imagine what it must be like to have to give such grim news on a regular basis.

Charlie glanced at his watch. 'I'm sorry I'm going to have to leave. I'm racing at Wetherby today.'

DCI Jordan gave him a grim nod and walked back to his car.

Charlie didn't feel in the least like riding, but he realised it was exactly what Will would have wanted. As he was about to leave his iPhone beeped. He gaped at the message. It was from Will. For a brief moment, he was completely confused. There must have been some mistake and Will was obviously texting to explain himself and the reason for his disappearance. Then he thought that it was a bizarre message from beyond the grave. Hope gave way to despair as he remembered that the reception locally was so bad that sometimes it took up to four days for text messages to arrive. He stared at the contents and nearly dropped the 'phone in shock.

Need to speak to you. Think I know what's going on with RG. Will.

Chapter 13

Tara found that she was still on a high from Rose Gold's win and the whole experience and been so much more fun that she had ever expected. Her grandmother, Caroline, had also been delighted and had caught up with the race from Montevideo, where she was on location filming. She had sent her a text.

Marvellous win, darling. Knew dear Rosie would do it. If Indy runs would you like to go along if I'm still tied up here? I'm sure Charlie and Miles will keep you in the loop. Lots of love and kisses x

Tara had responded by saying that of course work permitting, then she certainly would love to go along. The colours, the smells, the vividness of the whole drama kept popping into her head and she found herself smiling. And then there was the whole Charlie thing. She found herself rather intrigued by him. He was so knowledgeable about horses and racing that she felt confident to ask him anything. It was such a different world to the academic one in which she was now training, that she found herself fascinated despite worrying about the effect racing could have on people like Simon Norton, for example. The psychologist in her was prepared to moralise and be sanctimonious, but the normal human side of her had to acknowledge that she hadn't had so much fun in ages. It was an intoxicating mix of drama, colour and adrenaline all rolled into one.

Tara prepared for her sessions with both Ruth Cummings and Simon Norton today and she was also going to observe a family therapy session, as a colleague was using the offices for her work. Prior to Ruth arriving, she sat and read her supervision notes from her tutor regarding the case. Tara reread them and resolved to try to unpick with Ruth what her safe parameters were and how she might be able to extend these. She read in her case notes that if her husband David accompanied her then that vastly alleviated her symptoms, so she was going to suggest that he be invited into the sessions at some point. The idea would be to see how far Ruth could advance into those situations that caused her the most problem with David as a lifeline, and then attempt to reduce his role by getting him to step back. This could be phased out gradually so that David would be there but out of sight, finally allowing him to be on the end of a mobile. Her tutor had felt the couple's relationship might be the key to understanding how Ruth's behaviour had persisted, despite her attending therapy for several years.

Ruth came in looking quite bright and dressed in a red knitted dress and black boots.

'So how have you been?'

'OK.' Tara looked at Ruth carefully. She twisted her hands together awkwardly and picked at her face. 'Well, Dave and I haven't been getting on too well, actually...'

Tara nodded. 'Is this something that you want to talk about today?'

Ruth nodded and looked the picture of misery despite her smart dress. Tears started to fall down her face, silently at first and then great sobs took over. Tara handed her a box of tissues and waited for the crying to subside.

'I think he wants to leave me... You see all this stuff is starting to get on his nerves. He calls me a headcase and ...' Ruth's lips began to tremble uncertainly. She gazed at Tara willing her to understand. 'I know he doesn't mean it. He just gets fed up having to go around with me and do all the shopping and be at my beck and call. He wants to know why I'm not getting any better...'

Tara mulled this over. Was this the normal behaviour of a man frustrated by his wife's inability to go out and about her everyday life, or was it more than that? It was very hard to tell. Most partners probably would feel like this, she realised.

'So how does it make you feel...'

Ruth trembled as her sobs began to subside. She clutched her handkerchief and dabbed at her eyes.

'Well, worried sick. You see, I think he might actually leave me. He's sometimes said this before, but this time I think he might just do it.'

'What makes you think that?'

'Because I don't blame him. There're the things we can't do together, things I can't do, that he has to help with. Life is passing me by.' Ruth gave Tara a look full of bleak despair. 'I just want to get better, be a normal person, you know, beat this bloody, sodding thing once and for all. Make the most of my life.'

'You sound quite angry there, Ruth.'

Ruth gave a sigh and then looked Tara in the eye. 'Of course, I bloody am. I'm ready to give this ruddy phobia a run for its money, kick it into touch, once and for all.' Ruth smiled at her own daring.

Tara smiled back, impressed. Now this anger was something new, but something she could definitely channel and use to propel Ruth forward. Tara felt it was a major breakthrough, actually.

'Well, we'd better get down to business then. There's no time to waste.'

After a productive session in which Tara felt she had made great headway in helping Ruth, she was eating a sandwich when Margaret, one of the admin staff, came rushing in, breathing heavily.

'There's someone to see you, Tara. I told him you were on your lunch and were busy all afternoon, but he absolutely insisted on waiting. He's in the waiting room. Do you want me to get rid of him?' Margaret stiffened, preparing to give him the sharp edge of her tongue.

'Did you get a name?'

Margaret shrugged. 'I asked but he didn't answer. Good looking though and smart. Shall I go back and ask again?'

Tara glanced at her watch. That might just delay things. 'No, no. I'll see him. It's quite alright.'

Tara finished her rather unappetising cheese and ham sandwich and stood up. Perhaps, it was Simon Norton, Ruth's husband or maybe the new client she had been allocated?

She pushed her way through the double doors into the waiting room and realised her mistake. She had missed the vital clue that the stranger was smart and good looking. There sitting on an orange plastic chair was Callum, dressed in his stylish navy suit. He stood up, his face eager, as soon as Tara walked in. Damn, she thought, contemplating doing an immediate about turn. She had walked straight into that one.

'Tara, please. I need to speak to you and since you wouldn't return my calls, this seemed to be the only option...' Tara took in his rather pale but handsome face. He looked awful, as though he hadn't slept in an age. 'Please let me take you for a coffee and we can talk things through...' His dark eyes looked so serious she immediately felt herself hesitate. She glanced at her watch.

'I've got thirty minutes but no more.'

'How have you been?'

Tara was sitting opposite Callum in the local Costa Coffee, sipping her latte. Callum stretched out his hand across the table to meet hers, but she drew away. He frowned.

'Look, I had to come and see you because you wouldn't answer my calls or the door to me. I just wanted to see you.' He looked tired and angry. Then he took a deep breath. 'Tara, I don't know what you think you heard that day when you rang, but I am not back together with Anna. We were just playing happy families for Alfie's sake, after everything he's been through.'

Tara suddenly felt very tired. 'I know that, of course you had to go back and be there for them both in the circumstances. I understand that. I'm not some kind of a monster, you know.'

Callum grinned and she could see hope rising in his eyes. 'So, do you... is there still a chance?'

Tara found herself struggling how to phrase the next part.

'But what I'm wrestling with is what you really feel about the situation. I'm not at all sure everything is completely over between you and Anna.' Tara felt a huge lump in her throat and realised to her annoyance that the tears were beginning to fall. 'God, I shouldn't be saying this to you, because in the end it's me who could lose out, but surely you should try and work things out? The way you talk about Anna, are you sure there isn't something to salvage from your marriage? Because if there is you need to do it for all our sakes.'

Callum looked around the café desperately, as if trying to find the answers in the brightly painted cafe walls. Time seemed to stand still. Tara breathed in the scent of the coffee mixed with caramel and fought the urge to pacify and soothe. Unsay what she had just said. It would be so easy to fall back into the relationship again. She was very tempted to take the easy route and blot out the uncomfortable questions she had in her head.

After a long pause, Callum again stretched his hand over table to meet hers. This time she didn't pull away.

'Listen. You can't presume to know how I feel or think about Anna. We had a good time together, she's a great girl and I would never regret having Alfie but that's it.' Callum gazed at her with blistering intensity, as though he was willing her to understand. A couple with a toddler brushed passed, glancing at them curiously.

Tara lowered her voice. 'I guess what I'm saying is please be honest with me. I don't know what happened between you and Anna, but both of you seem reluctant to divorce, you get along and I just wonder what the hell you are doing with me? I don't want to be the 'other woman', it's just not my style and after everything with Alfie and the speed with which you dashed off, not that I don't understand, I just want you to be really, really sure. I suppose it has brought home the enormity of your past ties.'

Callum's eyes were glittering partly from anger, but also with tears.

'Well, that's very noble of you, I'm sure,' he continued darkly. 'You knew I was still married and had a child when we first started seeing one another and now it's suddenly an insurmountable problem? I just don't get it. You say you understand and then you blame me for acting like any caring father would do!' He slammed down his cup and began shredding his paper serviette savagely.

Tara sipped her latte and tried to calm herself. She found she was shaking slightly as she watched his beautiful long fingers tearing into the paper. Something shifted inside her and she came to a decision. Perhaps, there was a compromise situation after all?

'How about we just keep in touch as friends and see where things end up. That way you can sort out what you really want.'

Callum beamed. It was like the sun coming out.

'Great. Well how about dinner on Wednesday then? As friends, of course,' he added.

Tara nodded slowly and tried to feel pleased. But instead she felt she had just made a huge miscalculation.

As she came back to the office deep in thought, she noticed Simon Norton waiting and chatting with an attractive blonde wearing heels, a tight skirt and huge red scarf. Presumably, his wife? She glanced at her watch and realised he was early. She just had time to pop to the ladies.

When she invited him into his session, Simon Norton smiled expectantly at her. She observed that he was wearing a much better fitting and expensive looking suit and his watch looked new and designer like. She wondered vaguely where the money had come from, then dismissed her suspicions. Perhaps, he'd had a birthday or something? She shouldn't automatically jump to the wrong conclusions.

'How have you been this week?'

'Yeah, cool, OK really.'

Tara nodded, and Simon wriggled in his seat. Tara felt some disquiet as she had identified a clear link between this behaviour and avoidance.

'So, how did the diary linking your thoughts, feelings and behaviour go then?'

Simon gave her a blank look.

'Well, to tell you the truth I haven't really been doing it. And I have had a large bet.' He looked momentarily guilty then defiant.

Tara waited for him to say more. He continued to squirm, so she decided to rescue him.

'Well, you will have relapses, of course. I hope you didn't lose a lot of money.'

Simon shuffled in his chair and smiled. 'Well, that's just it, I didn't lose, I had a spectacular win, so I just came to tell you really. I heard about a hot betting tipster from one of me mates. He had some inside information. Of course, I had to pay to get the info, but it turned out amazingly well.' He grinned showing off his small white teeth. 'So fantastic in fact, I won't be coming back, you see. There's plenty more tips where that came from. Even the wife thinks I might make a professional gambler. Won £25,000 on a horse at Market Rasen in the fourth race. 25-1 it was! 'Simon was getting increasingly more animated and excitable. 'Bloody great, it were. Get in, you beauty! 'Simon stood up as he punched the air as though reliving the experience.

Tara felt the room start to spin a little. She had a horrible feeling.

'When was this and what race was it?'

Simon looked slightly surprised at her question and then a worried look passed over his face.

'The fourth race at Market Rasen, did you say?' Tara persisted. She had to find out. Simon flushed.

'Might have been, or was it Doncaster? That's right. It was a treble and two of the other horses were non runners,' he winked, as though this was dodgy, 'so all the money automatically went on the one horse to win.' He looked at Tara's stunned expression. 'No hard feelings, yeah? But I won't be coming back. I'm going to try and make it as a professional gambler. So, thanks but no thanks if you get my meaning.'

Tara stood up and managed to mutter some platitudes as he left. Then she sat at her desk for a moment trying to take it in. The words, inside information, betting tipster and fourth race at Market Rasen whirled round her mind. Then she remembered Charlie talking urgently to Miles directly after the race and felt her stomach drop. How many race meetings were there on Saturday and how many winners would there have been in the fourth race at 25-1? It had to be Rose Gold he was talking about. She reached for her mobile and scrolled down to Charlie's number. Just what the hell was going on?

Chapter 14

Charlie had mechanically gone through the motions at Wetherby and found that by trying not to think too much about Will's death and just blocking it out, he could manage to get through the day after a fashion. He had several rides and the regularity and routine helped him through. Even his old mate Tristan Davies commented on his quietness, however.

'What's up with you, Charlie? You've hardly said a word.'

They were getting changed at the end of the racing where Charlie had a reasonable day, but Tristan had had a winner and been placed. Strange how horses picked up on your mood, Charlie thought, thinking he'd have probably been placed on one of his rides at least in different circumstances. Charlie glanced around. Only Derek Jones remained in the weighing room, his eyes watchful in his pale face, as he packed up his kit bag.

Charlie lowered his voice. 'Well, there's been a death at the yard. Will Mellor was found having crashed off the Walton to Thornley Road. He came off the road in his car at Blackthorn Hill and hit a tree. He died instantly.'

'Gosh mate, that's terrible.' Tristan ran his fingers through his blond hair and frowned. The horse community was quite small and tight knit, and Tristan knew Will by reputation and by sight.

'I presume it was a horrible accident?'

Charlie glanced round. Derek was just leaving. He raised his arm to both. Charlie merely nodded. He paused making sure that Derek had definitely gone.

'Well, there's been some strange stuff going on at the yard lately. I'm not sure what the guvnor is up to or whether he is even aware. He's alright Miles, but he's quite remote and bangs on about how technology can help racing. He spends too much time on his laptop and not enough with the lads or the horses, if you ask me.' It felt quite strange to articulate what he was really thinking, Charlie realised, but quite liberating too.

'What do you think is going on then?'

Charlie shrugged. 'I'm not sure. But do you remember that horse that Caroline Regan bought for her granddaughter? Rose Gold, he's called. It's the strangest thing but he ran like a donkey on the gallops, really one paced and then on Saturday when I rode him at Market Rasen he was like a different animal, full of running. Won quite easily.' Charlie frowned. 'And two of our horses were withdrawn that day for lameness that seemed to come on very quickly.'

Tristan moved his head from side to side, as though weighing up the information that Charlie had given him.

'But you know as well as I do that some horses are lazy at home and only come into their own on race day. And some forms of lameness can only be apparent in some circumstances and appear very suddenly.'

Charlie considered this. 'But when you think that we've also had a lot of new staff lately, including a new vet, then I'm starting to wonder. And then I received this, after we heard that Will had died.' He fished in his pocket for his mobile and showed Tristan the text from Will. 'I'm wondering if Will put two and two together and...'

Tristan read the text. 'Met with a nasty accident. Christ, Charlie. What are you going to do?'

'Have a quiet word with Miles and see what he's got to say, I suppose…'He had been unable to do anything today as Miles had remained at the yard and was awaiting another visit from the police and one from Will's wife. Mick, the travelling Head Lad had had to deputise instead.

'Do you think it's some sort of drugs thing?' continued Tristan. 'At least Rose Gold should be tested for that. I presume he was picked up for a urine test after the race? So, it should come to light. Surely Miles wouldn't be so crazy as to get mixed up in anything illegal?'

'Yeah, he was picked up by the stewards due to his long odds.' Charlie's head was swimming. 'But Miles would have expected that, so I can't see it, at all. Perhaps, I'm overthinking things? I'll speak to Miles and see what he says. Perhaps, Will got the wrong end of the stick and maybe RG doesn't mean Rose Gold but refers to something else.' He racked his brains trying to think of what else it might mean but drew a blank. Charlie picked up his kit bag. A terrible thought occurred to him. Just supposing Miles was involved in some horse doping, would confronting him now mean that he might meet with the same fate as Will? Deep in thought he walked back to his car with Tristan as they threw ideas back and forwards. Then he noticed he'd had some missed calls from Tara. He didn't want to ring her back now as his head was a mess. He would ring her later.

'Can I have a word?'

Miles smiled ruefully. 'Yes, yes of course, come in. How are you? Terrible business all this stuff about Will. I've been speaking to the police and Linda, Will's wife.' His face was ashen. 'The police will want to take a formal statement from you. He seemed to confide in you about his feelings about his separation and lack of contact with his children, though I don't think it is suicide but apparently, they are looking at all angles. I wish I had listened and done more.'

Charlie took this in. Possible suicide? No. He would never have thought Will capable of that. He too wished he could have done more to help Will, though.

'Listen. Will sent me this message obviously before he died but I only received it this morning. It gave me quite a turn, but you know what the reception is like here.' Charlie tapped on the keys of his mobile and showed the message to Miles, who looked at it blankly. 'Do you have any idea what it might mean?'

Miles looked completely baffled and shook his head. 'Think I know what's going on with RG,' he repeated. 'Who or what is RG?'

Charlie cleared his throat. 'Well. Here's what I'm thinking. RG could be Rose Gold. You have appointed a lot of new people recently, Mick, Trevor and Alistair Morgan, the new vet.' Miles opened his mouth to object, but Charlie pressed on. 'How much do you know about them or trust them?'

Miles looked momentarily defiant and then hurt.

'Well, they all came highly recommended from Lawrence Prendergast, that's true. But hang on a minute, what are you trying to say?'

Charlie wondered how best to play it and decided to lay his cards on the table.

'Do you remember what I said directly after Rose Gold won his race about it being a bit too good to be true. Weren't you a tiny bit surprised about his change in form? I know I bloody well was.'

Miles' face darkened. 'Just what are you accusing me of exactly? Out with it!'

'Look, I'm not accusing you of anything, but supposing Alistair injected Rose Gold with something to make him run better...'

'Alistair wasn't there. And anyway, how could he have done that without anyone noticing and there is the small matter of the routine drugs tests. How is he supposed to get around that? Just think what you're saying, Charlie.'

Charlie looked at Miles his resolve floundering. 'Well, what about Mick or Trevor then? They have stopped the other lads going to the races, which is rather odd, don't you think? Why have they done that? Perhaps, they did something to enhance Rose Gold's performance?'

Miles shook his head. He hesitated, seemingly wondering how much to say.

'I see what you're saying but what you don't realise is that I asked them to take over the travelling part of the job exclusively, but not make it obvious. Hence the blanket approach. It's to do with Davy. He is a great lad and loves the horses but... Look, this is strictly confidential. I was given some information about Davy's behaviour at the race, so it was me that asked Mick and Trevor take over the race day stuff to save our reputation.'

'Right, OK. What was he getting up to?'

Miles grinned ruefully. 'Well, a reliable source told me that he and Rosie from Langley's yard have been meeting up at the races and, ahem,' Miles flushed, 'using the racecourse as an excuse to meet up and conduct their relationship.' Charlie knew Rosie quite well. She worked for a nearby racing yard and was a rather attractive brunette.

'Oh. Isn't Rosie married?'

'Yes, absolutely and as travelling head girl then she would always be at the races and very often at the same ones as us. So, it seemed a good way to stop Davy in his tracks.' Miles' face was flushed.

'So how do you mean conduct their relationship?'

'For Christ's sake Charlie, do you want a bloody diagram? They were seen in Langley's bloody horsebox having it off! I wouldn't mind but it was in work's time and they were so oblivious they were late getting the horses ready and damned near missed the race...'

Charlie smirked at the picture Miles had conjured up. Miles looked serious. 'Look. I'm sorry I didn't tell you about that, but as you can see, I wanted to keep that confidential, so don't breathe a word to anyone. And as for the rest of it, look I trust Alistair implicitly and if there's anything untoward, which I am sure there isn't, then it will come out in the drugs test.'

Charlie breathed a sigh of relief. 'Well, I just had to air my concerns that's all...'

Miles beamed.

'Quite right too. But there's nothing to worry about. I think Will's death has poleaxed us all, poor devil.' Miles stood up abruptly, rubbing his hands together. 'Look. We are going to have a great season despite this set back, I just know it. I do realise I'm new to all this and have a lot to live up to with my old man. But we can do it if we all pull together. Let's have a Scotch and a good old chinwag and clear the air.' He pulled out two glasses and poured a hefty serving of Scotch in each. Charlie sipped the amber liquid enjoying the fiery effect, as it made its way down his throat.

Something nagged away at his brain, telling him that something wasn't quite right but he ignored it. Probably it was a combination of the grief he felt for Will, bringing back the horrible feelings of guilt that resurfaced every so often. It was the anniversary of Helena's death combined with his anger at his mother's revelations about Jimmie Bird, he told himself. He picked over this wound and then gave up trying to understand his mother. It was just too bloody painful. For now, he told himself, the oblivion of alcohol was just what he needed.

He wasn't racing the next day, which was just as well, given the amount of Scotch he had drank. He scrambled around for two paracetamols and went out early to help the yard staff. It seemed that Mick had set everyone to work and there was little to do so he decided to school Rose Gold and another green horse called Candlewick. The yard had a paddock with several hurdle fences in it, away from the main gallops and it was still possible to form a loop which was long enough to gallop round. Rose Gold performed well over the hurdles and was a capable and careful jumper, but as he pushed him into a gallop

Charlie was still left with nagging doubts. Again, the horse lacked acceleration. At home, Rose Gold just did not measure up to his performance on the racecourse and Charlie was struggling to understand why. But he put his lack of speed down to his own groggy state of mind and dismissed it.

Later, a white car drew into the yard and a plain clothed detective knocked on the door. He had come to interview Charlie about Will. The man was probably about seven or eight years older than him and introduced himself as DI Blake. He wore a grey suit, wore his dark hair very short and had an expressive, mobile face.

'It shouldn't take too long. I've been allocated as the DI on the case now whilst DCI Jordan is heading up another case,' he said as Charlie led him back to his cottage and offered him a cup of tea.

DI Blake took notes longhand in lovely, italic print. He asked how long Charlie had worked at the yard, how long he knew Will, when he'd last seen him and the nature of the exchanges. As Charlie explained about Will's marriage break up and his frustration about the lack of contact with his children, the detective made copious notes and tapped the end of his pen thoughtfully.

'Do you think it was an accident or suicide even?' Charlie asked. 'Surely not suicide? I can't think of anyone less likely to take their own life. He was a tough old nut, Will. I can't imagine anything would get him down to that degree.'

DI Blake nodded. 'Well, sometimes you can't tell. It's often those that seem the least likely who do go through with it. But we are keeping an open mind and have appealed for witnesses. It's quite a remote spot though and most people go the other way around on the newer road, but you never know, someone might have seen something.'

'I did go looking for him on the evening. But it was dark and there was a slight fog up on the top there. I thought he might be in The Yew Tree in Walton. I did call at his house first and there was no sign of him.'

DI Blake chewed the end of his pen. 'What time would that have been, would you say?'

'Oh, about nine by the time we'd finished off in the yard, I'd say. We all stayed to help out.'

'Can I ask you about Mr Mellor's vehicle,' DI Blake read from his notebook, 'a navy blue five year old Astra, was it well maintained, did it have any signs of a recent accident, anything like that? Only there was some damage to the car, but it could have happened before.'

Charlie thought for a bit. 'Will was usually quite sensible. I'm sure he would have maintained it, but I suppose with everything that was going on, perhaps things slipped?'

DI Blake took a sip of his tea. 'And can you recall seeing any signs of a recent accident, damage that sort of thing, or did Will mention anything to you about that?' Charlie thought back to the last few weeks. Will's car had been parked at the side if the stables as usual and he had never thought to look at it really. It was pretty much always there, like Will he realised, a permanent fixture that everyone took for granted. Until it was gone. Why was Blake asking these questions?

'You don't think it was an accident, do you?'

For a second DI Blake hesitated but then pressed on with the party line. 'I can't possibly answer that now, but as I say, we are pursuing various lines of inquiry at the present time.'

Charlie had the feeling that Blake wasn't telling him everything. Then he remembered about Will's mobile.

'Oh, by the way, did you find Will's 'phone, by any chance?'

DI Blake flicked back through his pocketbook. 'I don't believe we did, sir.'

Charlie pulled his iPhone out of his pocket and scrolled down through his messages. 'Because I received this. It arrived after we heard about Will, due to the crap reception out here. Half scared me to death, actually.'

DI Blake peered at the screen and took down the content of the message.

'Does it mean anything to you? Who is RG, do you have any idea?'

For a split-second Charlie wondered about confiding in him about Rose Gold and his suspicions, but Miles had completely explained them all away, hadn't he? He had no evidence whatsoever. He looked back at the detective.

'No,' he found himself answering. 'I have absolutely no idea who RG is.'

As soon as she arrived home, Tara had leafed through the racecard she had kept from Market Rasen and used the internet to search the winners and odds. Then she searched for all the other race meetings held last Saturday. There were several. Bangor-on-Dee, Newcastle and Newbury. She pored over the results. There were no winners at 25-1 apart from Rose Gold. Mercy Me had come in at Bangor at 12-1 in the second and Equatorial had won at Newcastle at 10-1. If Simon had the day right and the odds, which she was sure he would have, then it was definitely Rose Gold he had bet on. Tara just couldn't make sense of it and tried Charlie's 'phone again. This time he picked up and they arranged to meet that evening. She arrived at the bar and decided to get straight to the point.

'Look, I've come to you first because my grandmother obviously has great faith in you, otherwise she wouldn't have asked you to help me with Rose Gold. I could speak to Miles, but I haven't for that reason. It's just when one of my clients tells me he won loads of money on the winner of the fourth race at Market Rasen due to 'insider information' and a tip he paid for, then it's not unreasonable to suspect something strange is going on.'

Tara and Charlie were sitting in a bar in York. She looked at him carefully, noticing the dark shadows under his eyes and taking in his desolate expression. He had explained there had been a death at the yard. Perhaps, she should have just left things? He was clearly in a bad way.

'Look, I realise this is not a great time, so perhaps we should talk about it later?' Tara had been coming into York anyway to meet Callum, so had thought she could kill two birds with one stone and talk to Charlie too. He seemed very preoccupied and was still in shock.

Charlie took a sip of his tonic water.

'I presume you have checked other race meetings to see if there was another winner at those odds, on that day?'

Tara nodded. 'Of course, I have. Sim... my client told me that he had had a treble and the other horses had been withdrawn which meant that all the money he had bet on the others went on the remaining runner. He won a load of money and now thinks he can have a career as a professional gambler and has stopped treatment. But that aside, I want to know just what is going on with my horse? Is the yard involved in something illegal? Tell me what you know.'

Charlie sighed. 'Well, I don't **know** anything for definite.'

Tara studied him. He was definitely holding out on her.

'But you do suspect something is going on?'

Charlie nodded, glumly. 'I'll get another round in and tell you everything I know.'

He went through the whole story from Rose Gold's poor form at home, to the changes in staff that Miles had introduced which included Mick, Trevor and the vet Alistair Morgan. Then he explained about Will, his misgivings about the yard, his death and then the text he had sent. Tara's face was an absolute picture. He also went on to explain his discussion with Miles and how he had managed to explain everything away.

'So, you see, Miles did have a valid reason for letting Mick and Trevor take over the travelling side of the yard and Rose Gold could just be one of those horses that only become psyched up on the race course.'

Tara nodded thoughtfully. 'But what about my client and him letting slip the fact that he had inside information that he paid for? Doesn't that strike you as odd?'

Charlie scratched his head. 'Well, there are always unscrupulous types who try to sell foolish people betting tips. I believe in the ultimate integrity of the sport and there are a lot of checks and balances in place to keep it clean. Perhaps, he was just lucky?'

Tara studied Charlie carefully. 'So, assuming Will's death was an accident and Rose Gold only performs on the racecourse and my client got lucky then there's nothing to worry about?' Charlie nodded and smiled.

'But the worst case scenario is that Rose Gold's performance was enhanced, Will found out about it and was murdered to shut him up and a person or persons unknown are involved in doping horses. My bloody horse in particular.'

'Yes, that's about the size of it.'

Tara frowned, her delight in Rose Gold's win had been irretrievably sullied. And that made her angry. 'Well, we should definitely involve the police. That's my view, absolutely.'

'The police are investigating Will's death already, so perhaps we should just let them get on with their job.'

Tara considered this. 'And they know about the text message Will sent you?'

Charlie nodded. She took in his blue eyes with thick, dark lashes which were impossibly gorgeous. She even felt a moment's disloyalty to Callum. No wonder he was the pin up boy of National Hunt racing.

Charlie sighed. 'So, we just sit tight and keep our eyes open.'

No bloody way, Tara thought. She was involved now because of Rose Gold and she was damned well going to see this through to the bitter end. She couldn't just leave it. She would do some digging even if it was just over the internet. But there was no need to tell Charlie that. He was gazing at her intently.

'But say nothing to anyone, do you understand, because if there is something dodgy going on, and it's a big if, then we could be in danger.

Tara bit her lip. She had been hoping to discuss things with Callum to get a good legal brain on the job. Or possibly her grandmother who had started the whole thing by buying her Rose Gold in the first place.

Charlie looked around the bar and lowered his voice. 'I mean it, Tara. It's important. Very important. We should keep in touch, too. Is that OK?'

Tara nodded and realised he was deadly serious. She looked at his stern expression and found she rather liked the fact that he was looking out for her. A frisson of anticipation flashed through her, mingled with fear.

'Well, I have to go, anyway. I'm meeting someone.' Tara glanced at her watch and took another sip of her drink. Charlie was looking at her curiously.

'You know you can tell me to mind my own business, but this relationship you're in doesn't seem to be making you very happy...'

She felt as though she'd been slapped. 'What? Look, you know nothing about Callum or me for that matter,' she snapped. 'I thought you were here to talk about racing. I think you've overstepped the mark.' Tara saw the hurt in Charlie's eyes.

He gave her a half smile. 'No. You're right.'

Tara pulled on her coat. 'Look. I've got to go, and I won't tell a soul, I promise. I'll be in touch.'

Charlie stretched out his hand to clasp hers. 'OK. But be careful, promise me.'

She nodded. It seemed that nothing had changed between them but at the same time everything had. Somehow, it wasn't just about the investigation anymore, things were blurring between them, boundaries softening. A group of girls behind Charlie were preening themselves and watching them with interest. They were ready to pounce as soon as she left. Charlie drained his glass and ignored them.

'I'll come out with you. I could do with an early night.' He picked up his coat. 'And just so you know I wanted to meet you, it wasn't just because Caroline asked me to.' With that Charlie pulled up his collar and walked away.

Tara walked in the opposite direction to Candles Wine bar to meet Callum, her head reeling from everything he had told her. And as for that last bit? Well, he certainly seemed sincere. She tried to examine her feelings towards Callum. Perhaps, Charlie was right? Then she turned her thoughts to the Rose Gold issue. Damn, she had forgotten to pick his brain about the fact that Simon had told her he had a treble. Surely, that was significant? Hadn't Miles had some other runners that had to be withdrawn? That certainly pointed to a betting scam, especially if those two horses in the tip off were from Miles' yard. Still, she would need to know what other bets Simon had had and since he wasn't likely to be coming back then it was going to be impossible to find out. She reached the street where the bar was situated and trudged on in her heels, wrapping her coat around her. There were a few people about and the entire country was revving up for Christmas, she realised lights, Christmas trees, snowmen and reindeer already visible on many of the shop fronts, pubs and bars and it wasn't even quite December yet.

Callum was waiting for her, looking resplendent in an expensive grey suit, his black, wool coat folded up on the seat next to her. She saw him before he realised she was there. He glanced at his watch and frowned. It had been such a brief time since her birthday party when she had been given her present, Rose Gold, but she realised that something had shifted inside her. A few weeks ago, she would have been delighted to see Callum and she would have felt sick with excitement and anticipation. Now she felt none of those things. Instead, Charlie's words rang in her ears. Callum looked up and saw her. He was half smiling and half frowning because she was late. She felt a flicker of annoyance at his expression and an invisible pull back to the man she had had previously met and the intriguing story he had told.

'You just don't seem with it, darling? What's wrong?' Callum asked when he had repeated himself several times to get any sort of rational response from her.

'Oh, I'm just tired,' she told him. Later she explained that she needed her rest and would go home alone. Really, she needed some time to think things through. If Callum was there, then she would be so tempted to confide in him. Callum tried to hide his hurt feelings, but then smiled and gave her a chaste kiss on the forehead.

'Of course, Tara. You look exhausted. I'll ring you in the week.'

Tara tried to disguise a yawn as the team meeting droned on. Team meetings were usually once a week and stuck to a rigid agenda that was not inspiring. The team leader, Matt Ferguson was trying to referee a 'discussion' between Naomi and Gwen, two of the psychologists in the team. The debate was about 'inclusivity' apparently and Naomi was querying the wisdom of putting up the rather shabby Christmas tree to decorate the drab waiting area. Naomi felt that this should be debated as she thought it might alienate the ten or so service users who were from different ethnic backgrounds and who might have different religious beliefs. Matt had resignedly suggested they study the ethnic and religious breakdown of their service users to help them make a decision. One of the staff, Alison who compiled this information, had volunteered to print it out and Matt was studying the data. Matt was in his forties, sandy haired and a little balding. He struggled to deal with some of the squabbles and undercurrents that are present in most office environments. Naomi was looking mutinous and self righteous, whilst Gwen feigned boredom. Tara doodled in her notebook and tried to focus.

'Well,' Matt announced, looking round the table. 'Of those who consented to giving us the information regarding their ethnicity which is 99%, only 6% of those are of a different ethnicity.' Matt's chunky finger went down the statistics. 'And of those 5%, all are 'white British and other', which leaves just 1% of service users being of a completely different ethnicity. And there is a similar picture for religious beliefs. So, given the numbers then I suggest we still display our traditional Christmas tree in the foyer as usual. I'm sorry Naomi, but the numbers just don't warrant taking this stance.' Margaret, the senior administrator glanced at Naomi nervously whilst Gwen smiled triumphantly. There were murmurs of approval whilst Naomi simply pursed her lips very tightly.

'Any other business, anyone?'

Margaret produced a brightly coloured, red scarf and umbrella from under the desk.

'Ahem, these were found in the reception area last week. Does anyone know who they belong to? Otherwise, they'll end up at the charity shop...'

Tara looked up, startled. Wasn't that the scarf that Simon Norton's wife had been wearing?

'Yes, I know who the scarf belongs to. It's fine, I'll make sure they get it back,' she bluffed.

She was delighted, as she now had the perfect opportunity to contact Simon Norton again. The office would have a record of his home address and she could always make out she was just passing. She looked at her notebook and realised that she had doodled a picture of a horse. God, what was happening to her? Rose Gold, his win and all the questions this had thrown up had started to dominate her thoughts. She really must get a grip.

Chapter 16

Charlie had a few runners at Doncaster that afternoon, so after riding on the gallops, he intended on making some inquiries of his own before setting off for the racecourse. The conversation with Tara had completely rocked him to the core and although he had been careful to tow the party line and trot out the reassurances that Miles had given him, he was becoming increasingly uneasy about what he had heard and what it all meant. Tara. He found himself wondering about her increasingly these days too. He was unsure who to trust and decided that until he had information to the contrary, everyone was under suspicion. Since news of Will's death, the yard seemed to have had the life sucked out of it and all the staff were edgy, suspicious and unhappy. Davy and Neil were gossiping with Fay, a new lass who had been brought in to help but the tone, which was usually jocular, was now flat and anxious. Mick and Trevor, to give them their due, had stepped in and worked masses of overtime to keep the yard going. Mick ran a tight ship but also worked just as hard if not harder than any of them. Even Miles had taken to getting up early and mucked out a few stables before breakfast which was unheard of. But the reality of Will's death and the questions it raised hung over the place like a toxic fog. He felt that there was a real possibility that something untoward was going on and Will had found out. It was possible that this had led to his murder.

Once he had untacked his mounts, he had an hour or so to spare so he decided to drive up to Blackthorn Hill and revisit the site of the crash. As he drove, although cold, the sun was shining, and he felt relieved to be out of the yard and the claustrophobic atmosphere. He approached the hill then decided to park up in one of the passing places, set up due to the narrowness of the road and walk the rest of the way. This meant he could take his time and study the area very closely. He didn't want to miss anything. As he climbed the hill, Tara's words came back to him. Although, to her he had dismissed her client's bet as just a fluke, he was fairly sure it was far from that. Something must have been given to Rose Gold to make sure he performed on the day and somehow Tara's client had happened upon that information. But who was involved? The list of suspects was endless, and he was struggling coping with this. Miles, Alistair, Mick, Trevor, the lads? Anyone of them could be involved. And if Will had found out what was going on and then been killed as a result, then the stakes must be huge.

He continued to climb to where the road narrowed, and the track fell sharply on the descent into the rocks below, through heather and scrub land. His heart pounded as he saw the tyre tracks still visible in the heather, making their way to a substantial area where the plants were heavily depressed in front of a large tree. This was clearly the crash site although the car had long since been moved. Judging from the size of the area it was possible that Will had lost control on the descent and plunged headlong downhill. The car may even had flipped over. He looked for tyre marks. There were some on the road at right angles to the drop, but also on the other side of the road near the entrance to Blackthorn Hill Farm. It was hard to know if they were recent or not. He dismissed them anyway, as surely any tracks would be initially parallel to that side of the road but veering off towards the edge of it? Charlie looked around him at the bleak area and felt guilt and grief consume him. There was still the possibility that Will had taken his own life or that he had been drunk and accidentally steered off course. Either way he felt he owed it to Will to do everything in his power to find out what had happened. He wished he could turn back time and spend longer listening to him about his problems. But that wasn't going to happen and thinking like that was going to lead nowhere, he realised.

Virtually opposite the drop, was the entrance to Blackthorn Hill Farm. He walked over and looked at the old gates and the *Danger-Keep Out* sign daubed in red paint. He remembered old Mr Price very warmly, as he had been kind enough to give him a few good rides as a conditional, when he was starting out. He had gone down there to do some schooling, so knew the place when it was a thriving farm and stables. Now the rusty gates were closed shut and he had no idea what had happened to the property upon the old man's death. He walked up to the gates and fingered the substantial lock and chain that held them secure. Although the gates were old, the lock was new and looked like it was kept well oiled. And when he looked beyond the entrance it was clear that there were signs of recent tyre tracks which led on to the road. He made a mental note to ask what was going on with the property. Perhaps, the delay in the sale had been something to do with Probate and now things were finally sorted out? He recalled the farm had a reasonable set of brick built stables and the benefit of an uphill gallop which was very useful for training purposes. It would be great if it could be brought back to life. As he walked, he passed the blue police sign which had been erected, asking for witnesses to the crash to contact the local police station. Given the geography of the road, although it was a more direct route to Walton, many motorists he guessed preferred the longer route, which at least included an 'A' road and no steep inclines or descents. So, most people would take the longer but much quicker route, so he was unsure if anyone would have witnessed the crash. He had a horrible feeling that 'accidental death' would be the conclusion of the Coroner unless there was any other evidence. He wondered what had happened to Will's 'phone? Perhaps the police had found it at his home and that might reveal something further? He left trying to dispel his sombre mood and concentrate on the day's racing.

He arrived at Doncaster in good time and managed to have a chat with Tristan and discuss the latest revelations. Tristan, similarly, was of the opinion that the information from Tara was deeply significant.

'Suppose it's one of the gang, probably someone lower down the pecking order trying to make a fast buck by selling tips? Did you hear of that case recently where punters were conned by being given tips on fixed races, and then once they had confidence in the system they were encouraged to buy into the betting system by paying a heavy fee and lost the lot, of course. The race fixing just gave the illusion of a fool proof betting system. But you and I know there's no such thing.'

'Yeah, it's an old, old con but punters still fall for it.'

'How are the police doing with the investigation into Will's death?'

'Not sure. I have been interviewed and showed them the text he sent me, but they were tight-lipped. Suppose they have to be...'

Tristan nodded. 'Anything from Rose Gold's drug test?'

'No, not a thing so far.'

Tristan scratched his head. 'Do you suppose this new vet chappie is up to something? I suppose vets could be one step ahead of the drugs testing? I mean there are new substances coming out all the time.'

'Yeah, that's right.' Charlie thought about this. Perhaps, that was it. 'The new vet is a chap called Alistair Morgan. He's a young, studious looking guy. Have you heard anything about him?'

Tristan thought for a bit. 'Nope. But I'll ask about and I do have a mate who is a Private Investigator. He was an ex-cop but still has loads of contacts that might help. I can give you his number.'

'Great.'

Derek Jones walked in at that point and smiled ingratiatingly at them.

'Now then, gentlemen. How are we today? Do you fancy your chances, then? '

He was wearing a smart suit and when he put down his kit bag, a shiny watch flashed from his wrist. Was that a Rolex, Charlie wondered? Then he dismissed the thought. It was probably a fake. Derek was pretty much small fry in the national hunt jockeys' ranking and certainly couldn't afford any such luxury by Charlie's reckoning. That was unless he was earning money by other means, of course.

'I was up you neck of the woods the other day. Lovely countryside. I wouldn't mind settling there myself. What do you say? Give you gentlemen a run for your money, hey?'

'Be our guest,' countered Charlie with a smile. Increasingly Derek was at more of the northern race meetings, he realised. He and his agent's aggressive style of getting rides had probably ruffled a few too many feathers down south, he reckoned. He had nothing to fear from the likes of Derek Jones.

'That's right. We always welcome healthy competition, don't we Charlie?' continued Tristan who was obviously feeling the same. For a second, Derek lifted his chin and appeared about to challenge them. Then he thought better of it and smirked.

'I don't think I'm quite in your league yet, but give me time gentlemen, give me time...'

Charlie was about to remark that even if he had a hundred years, he still didn't think he'd ever be a real contender but thought better of it. He wondered idly what Derek was doing in Yorkshire, then dismissed the thought. Derek Jones was a nobody, someone who just wasn't worth getting annoyed about, he told himself.

Charlie had two rides for Miles and two for Laura Palmer, the female trainer. Charlie was riding Zorba the Greek the youngster who was very promising and the older Madding Crowd. He was engaged to ride a couple of youngsters for Laura but as she was such a good horsewoman this did not worry him as much as it should. Racing youngsters was a risky business, but he trusted Laura and knew she would have schooled her horses meticulously.

Miles met him in the parade ring looking rather flustered.

'The horses have only just arrived in the nick of time,' he muttered. 'Had to come in the old box as the new one is in the garage.' Like many yards they had moved onto one of the smaller, newer two horse lorries which were much nippier, easier to handle and did not require the driver to hold an HGV licence. The old box was larger, for four horses and they still used it, but it was becoming increasingly decrepit and slow.

'Never mind. They're here now.' He pointed to Trevor who was leading the magnificent Zorba the Greek round the parade ring. 'Well, he's looking fit, but as it's his first race just take it steady and see how you go. There will be plenty of opportunities to win with this one, so don't rush him.'

Charlie touched his cap to the owners, a middle aged couple who were excited at the prospect of Zorba's race and the positive feedback they had received about him. Charlie felt the familiar thrill as he felt the power of the horse as he surged over each fence and despite his promise not to push Zorba, when the opportunity came up to win, he could not resist. Zorba seemed full of running and was handling the experience like a pro. He hadn't reckoned on Jake Horton's mount, though, and the two fought it out for first place, Charlie winning by a short head. Well, that cleared the cobwebs away, Charlie thought as he rode into the winner's enclosure, greeted by loud cheers. He was debriefing with Miles when he saw a pair of familiar eyes staring at him, set in a freckled, open face. Gina. She appeared to be smiling and applauding but when he looked again, she had gone. He hadn't seen her in ages and felt a pang of guilt at the manner of the separation. He resolved to find her later.

As ever with racing, there were highs and lows. The yard's veteran Madding Crowd which was favourite, came in second and his last mount,

Laura's Chameleon deposited Charlie in an ignominious heap at the fourth from last, having stumbled badly through the hurdle, pecking on landing. As the St John's ambulance men checked him over, he reflected that that was racing for you. Fortunately, his injuries were a horseshoe sized bruise on his left leg and some minor cuts and bruises, but nothing an ice pack wouldn't cure. He was transported back to the weighing room with a heavy heart.

He managed to catch up with Gina in the bar. She saw him and headed off in the other direction, but he ignored the pain in his leg and ran after her.

'Gina, Gina. Come and have a drink with me, come on.' She paused and shrugged.

'OK. OK. Don't make a spectacle out of yourself.'

Charlie grinned and ordered a dry white wine for her and a diet coke for himself.

'Look. I just wanted to say I'm sorry for the way things worked out. I had no idea you would leave so quickly without even saying goodbye.'

Gina sighed. 'Well, let's just say it was easier that way. I knew you'd talk me out of leaving.'

Charlie thought he probably would have. He felt suddenly at a loss for words. 'Anyway, you look well.' She did too. 'Where are you working now?'

'I took Rosie's old job at Smiths place, you know the travelling head girl job.'

Charlie nodded remembering what Miles had said about Davy and Rosie and their liaisons at the racecourse. Perhaps, her husband made her leave because of Davy?

'Oh, where's she gone then?'

'To the Midlands somewhere. She's been gone six months or so now. I went away for a few months then came back last week. Anyway, what is this,

Charlie? You hurt me, remember and I shouldn't really give you the time of day, if I had any sense.'

Charlie took in what she had said about Rosie being gone for six months. No, that couldn't be right, otherwise why had Miles taken action to stop Davy and Rosie's liaisons when she hadn't even been here for ages? He was about to ask Gina if she was sure and then noticed her flushed face and decided against it.

'Look, what do you want?'

Charlie wondered how to play it. 'Just to talk to you and see how you are. And to apologise...'

Gina shook her head. 'Well, you've done that now, but I don't really see us as being the best of mates now, do you?'

Charlie considered this. 'No, perhaps not. But I just wanted to say hello, that's all and see how you were doing. I do care about you, you know.'

Gina took a sip of her wine and gave rueful smile. 'But not enough, evidently.' She put her hand up. 'OK, OK Charlie boy. Have it your own way. Let's at least be civilised about things. Especially as I'm back in the area.'

Her gaze drifted to someone or something over his shoulder.

'So, I suppose you heard about Will?'

'What's he done now, the silly, old sod,' she said fondly.

She clearly hadn't then. Charlie took a deep breath. 'Gina, I'm afraid he died in a car accident a few days ago.'

The blood drained from Gina's face. 'God, poor Will, that's awful.' She was shocked but for a split second something else flickered over her face. Her eyes were drawn over his shoulder again. He turned his head and noticed Derek Jones sipping a drink with a couple of other men. Gina turned back to Charlie, her expression almost fearful. It was hard to know which had upset her most, the news of Will's death or the sight of Derek Jones.

Chapter 17

Tara was on placement for the half the week and spent the rest of the time in the University considering what to complete her Doctoral research on. Ruefully, she thought about betting systems or working with compulsive gamblers or horse doping, as she rifled through the journals at the Brynmor Jones Library at the University of Hull. It was no good, this issue of whether Rose Gold had won by fair means or foul was proving to be a huge distraction. She borrowed some books for her essay, which was due to be handed in soon, and spent the rest of the time using the internet to search articles about betting scams and scandals. She was amazed at the large number.

There were several common betting schemes and cons that the unwitting punter could fall prey to. She started to feel very worried about Simon Norton and what he might risk, and more than likely lose, if he was involved in something that later turned out to be illegal. There was a case a few years ago of businessman Bert Smith and his accomplice stable lad, Alun Jones who were wanted on suspicion of a betting scam. Bert had sent out lavish brochures, claiming that betting system was logical and with experience and knowledge it was entirely feasible that anyone could make a killing from professional gambling. The brochure depicted Bert's lavish home, model wife, yacht and all the trappings of wealth, he had claimed to make from gambling and the fictitious betting system. Alun was said to have worked at several stables in Epsom and given Bert inside information. Having fixed a couple of races, punters were confident in the system, so confident, amazingly many people had paid the 'one off' fee of five thousand pounds to be given an introduction into this gilded world, only to find that there were no more tips and the two had hightailed it with their money. There was a picture of them looking suitably sombre having been caught. Alun Jones was dark haired, blue eyed and looked incredibly young. How on earth had he got involved in all this, she wondered? He looked innocent and vaguely familiar though she didn't know why. Bert Smith, she read had been the brains behind the operation and he served a substantial seven year sentence whereas Alun Jones, due to being sixteen at the time of the offences, received a supervision order to be managed by the local Youth Offending Team. Supposing Simon Norton had fallen prey to a similar scheme? She made a mental note to contact Simon using his wife's scarf as an excuse to at least check that he was OK. However, she had to accept that as an adult he could choose his own path in life.

She also completed a search regarding illegal substances that enhanced athletic performance and found several articles about cyclists who trained using the banned substance EPO and discontinued use four days before a competition. The use during training was sufficient to allow them to push their bodies further and thus gave them an unfair advantage whilst racing. If usage was stopped at least four days before, it was untraceable in routine drugs testing. She wondered if there was something similar used in racing and shuddered at the thought. She was sure Charlie had mentioned that Rose Gold would have been tested, and that so far as she knew there had been no banned substances found. Still, it was a good place to start with the vet that Charlie had mentioned, so she searched for Alistair Morgan. There was very little information that she could find except a photo of an earnest looking, bespectacled young man who seemed to have excellent credentials. Surely such a man wouldn't jeopardise his reputation by getting involved in anything illegal? Baffled, she reluctantly shut down her laptop and made her way to her lecture. She was calling in on her parents later and Lawrence and Lola were invited, so perhaps that would help her get the whole thing into perspective. She was mindful about what Charlie had said to her not to discuss the case with anyone, but she has so many questions, this was going to be impossible. Perhaps, she could ask Lawrence about the integrity in racing without arousing suspicion? Still, she would hopefully get to see Charlie on Wednesday when Indian Ocean was racing again. She and her parents would accompany her to Haydock Park, as her grandmother was still away filming.

Her parents were delighted to see her. Mum was just pouring a gin and tonic as she prepared their meal, chicken with mustard sauce, and offered Tara a drink.

'So, how is the placement going? Do you have any interesting cases?'

'Yes. I'm working with a claustrophobic woman and a compulsive gambler and sitting in on some family therapy.'

Mum sipped her drink and said in hushed tones. 'Oh, how interesting. Your Uncle Lawrence used to have a little gambling problem, you know. Still, Lola soon sorted it out.' Her mother gave her a stern look. 'For goodness sake, don't say anything, will you.'

Tara nodded and took this in and was about to ask more questions when the doorbell rang heralding Lawrence and Lola's arrival.

Her father showed them in as they hugged everyone.

Tara found herself eyeing her uncle rather differently. Lawrence was a tall, distinguished looking man who was dressed in country casuals. Her aunt, Lola, was blonde with wavy hair and a big open smile. Tara found herself wondering how exactly she had sorted out Lawrence's 'little problem', as in her experience it was not easy, especially being as immersed as he was in the racing world. Lawrence was a Bloodstock Agent and supplied racehorses to select clients. His work took him to studs in England and abroad and he had an excellent reputation in being able to pick out future winners and of course he had an encyclopaedic knowledge of blood lines. She wondered how he could have kicked his gambling habit, when faced with such temptation and with such knowledge as he possessed.

'So, when is Rose Gold running again?' asked Lawrence when they were sitting down for the meal.

'Oh, quite soon, I think. He did perform wonderfully and didn't pick up any injuries,' replied Tara.

'Well, your uncle was bound to have selected an excellent specimen for you,' continued Lola. 'Nothing but the best for our darling Tara. Ma was absolutely clear about that.'

Tara smiled back. 'I don't know if it's the norm but apparently Rose Gold was picked for a urine test following his win.' Tara studied Lawrence, but he seemed completely unperturbed by this. 'Is that usual would you say?'

Lawrence finished his mouthful of food. 'Oh absolutely. Quite routine, I assure you. The stewards usually select which horses have urine tests and given his win and rather long odds then of course, he was always going to be selected. Splendid win, though. I even had a little bet myself.' Lawrence glanced at Lola. 'Just a tiny one. I should think you will do very well with him and have a wonderful time too, I'm sure. His bloodlines through his sire, Rose of Tralee are simply to die for.'

Tara decided to head Lawrence off from one of his bloodline monologues, knowing that if she didn't it could go on for rather a long time.

'So, do you think racing has a problem with drugs?' she asked.

There was a shocked silence

'No, no. Of course not. No more than any other sport, I should imagine. The racing authorities are very hot on that sort of thing as it just undermines public confidence, which in turn reflects very badly on the whole industry.'

Tara considered this. She had read about the British Horseracing Authority and they did seem to have a rigorous policy about these matters, even to the extent of randomly testing horses in training away from the racecourse. This had the effect of being able to spot any yards using banned substances whilst the horse was in training and not actually at the racecourse. Tara continued.

'Still, I suppose it would be entirely possible to be one step ahead of the tests, as it were. You know, manage to find something that would enhance a horse's performance but wouldn't appear in a test now.'

Lawrence nodded. 'I suppose theoretically then, yes. But really Tara, I should just enjoy Rose Gold and don't worry your pretty head about it.'

Her father, Jack was scowling at her. 'You mustn't mind Tara, Lawrence. I blame her University studies, it has certainly given her an unusually inquiring mind. Everything must be analysed and picked over.'

Lawrence smiled. 'Not at all. It's wonderful to find someone who takes such an interest.' However, he was looking slightly uneasy, Tara noticed. She was longing to talk further about gambling and so on, but her mother was giving her warning looks so she decided to move on to the safer topic of Indian Ocean's forthcoming race and Caroline's latest film. Her grandmother was playing the role of a female criminal mastermind in a Guy Ritchie film. She was hugely enjoying playing a glamorous baddie and getting her hands on guns and fast cars. It all sounded great fun and Tara couldn't wait to see it.

Later back in her house she reflected on what she had learned so far. Very little in the way of hard facts. It was clear that in general terms betting scams and horse doping scandals did happen, but also that there were many safeguards already in place. Yet someone had tipped Simon Norton off about her horse's performance. How could they have known about it? Although, promising on the flat, Rose Gold was little raced over hurdles and taken with his lacklustre performance at home and the other changes in personnel Charlie had told her about at the yard, her instincts told her something wasn't right. Although Charlie had been measured in what he had said, she knew that he had his suspicions too. And then there was the death of Will and his strange text to Charlie. Surely the RG mentioned in that could easily be Rose Gold? She made a list in a spare notebook and considered her next step. Then, she saw the scarf that Simon Norton's wife had left in reception where she had left it in the hallway. A visit to Simon Norton was most definitely in order. But how could she get him to reveal more than he intended, as he was bound to be extremely guarded? That was altogether a trickier question.

Chapter 18

Charlie arrived home to find the police had left a message on his answer machine asking him to get in touch regarding their inquiries. He made a note of the telephone number and fished out his ice packs. He had been patched up by the St John's ambulance staff and given pain killers, but now needed to set to work as the swelling on his leg was worsening. He made a chicken salad and settled down with his ice packs, a bottle of scotch and painkillers. Chameleon had certainly caught him well and truly on his leg and there were several other cuts and bruises that needed attention too.

He was just settling down to watch the TV when Nat appeared at his door. He looked pale and ill at ease. His face looked grey and his hair was almost white these days. He looked exhausted as news of Will's death had clearly hit him hard.

'Just thought I'd pop in with a bottle of Scotch. Saw you had a fall and thought you might need one and to be honest I wanted to have a chat about Will. I still can't bloody believe it, Charlie lad.' The old man's eyes were watering, and his face was grim. 'Bloody well ridden with that Zorba The Greek. Now he is one to watch!' He brightened at this prospect. Then he noticed the look on Charlie's face. 'I hope I'm not disturbing you?'

'No, of course not. You're quite alright. Great minds think alike. I was just about to have a drink anyway. Helps with the pain.'

They sat and sipped their Scotch in silence for a minute or two. Eventually Nat spoke.

'Bloody awful business. I know he spoke to you, Charlie, about his marriage breaking up and it must have been awful, but I can't see him taking his own life. Can you?'

'No, I have to admit, I can't. Is that what the police are saying now? I know he was a bit down, depressed even, but he was still fairly upbeat even though Linda was making it hard for him to see the kids. Apparently, they didn't want to see him.'

Nat took this in and nodded gravely. 'That must have hurt. I really don't know what the police's conclusion will be, but I just wanted to check with you. I feel responsible somehow. I know I'm not the guvnor now, but you never stop feeling responsible for people. I set him on twenty years or so ago. Skinny little lad he was then but full of spirit. Irrepressible really. Knew his wife Linda, too. They were so in love.' Nat sighed and drained his glass. 'I heard you got a strange text from Will.'

Charlie nodded, wondering if that was the real reason for the visit. He pulled out his 'phone, pressed some buttons and showed the text to Nat. The old man squinted his eyes to look.

'Does it mean anything to you?' Nat stared intently at Charlie.

Charlie shrugged. 'Well, I did wonder if RG was Rose Gold but now, I don't know. It could be anything really.'

Nat looked troubled. 'Did he say anything else to you, you know, before the accident?'

'Charlie shook his head. 'No, just about the kids and Linda. That was all really.' Charlie couldn't bring himself to mention that he had serious doubts about Miles' training methods.

Nat sniffed. 'Well. Look if there's anything I can do to help the lads and lasses, you will tell me, won't you? Must keep their morale up, you know.'

Charlie smiled. 'Of course, I will. Listen, do you want another?'

Nat shook his head. 'No, I mustn't with this ruddy ticker, you know. The doctors said I should have a bypass operation, you know. Might improve things but the truth is, I'm bloody scared of dying on the operating theatre, Charlie. It would be so bloody undignified, somehow.'

Nat looked at him, the fear, all too evident in his eyes.

'It's a fairly straightforward operation these days, isn't it? My grandfather had one and he was as right as rain. Maybe you should reconsider?'

Nat gave a weak smile. 'Perhaps, you're right, Charlie, perhaps, you're right. I'll talk it through with my consultant. Anyway, don't be a stranger. Do call in on us.'

Charlie agreed he would and showed the old man out. He then immersed his leg in a bucket of ice and gulped down another Scotch in the hope of deadening the pain. He had wanted to confide in Nat about his suspicions about Rose Gold and the possible betting scam, but he had thought better of it. The old man was no fool, though, and he wondered if he could well harbour some suspicions of his own.

The Scotch was taking effect as were the painkillers. He removed the ice pack from his leg and watched something mindless on the television. He went to bed in a strange mood, his head filled with questions to which he had no answers.

Kim was proving something of an asset at Thornley. A law student at York, she was a rather brusque dark haired girl with a capable and efficient manner. Her black painted nails, nose and facial piercings did make her look rather exotic in such traditional surroundings, but she had transformed Miles' home, whipped up some unusual but delicious cakes for the owners' visits and thoroughly organised Miles' rather esoteric filing and accounting systems. Her courgette cake was to die for, apparently. Charlie wondered how she had the time, but Miles had assured him that she only had a few hours lectures a week, so was able to spend lots of time at Miles' without eating into her study time.

Kim came in with steaming mugs of tea and toast.

'I'm done cleaning, so do you want me to start on these, Miles?'

'Hmm. Maybe make a start on the owners' bills, first?'

'OK. I'll set to.' Her eyes lingered briefly over Charlie for a second too long, but he was oblivious.

'Right, entries then, Charlie. How's the leg by the way? Stiff?'

Charlie shook his head. 'No, it's fine. It was a little stiff, but riding has definitely loosened it up.'

Miles nodded. 'Did dad come and see you?'

'Yes. He's very cut up about Will's death.'

'Of course. We all are.'

'So, I hear Zorba has a bit of heat in his off fore.' Fresh from his victory yesterday, Neil had been quite concerned about it and had discussed it on the gallops that morning.

'Well, Alistair is popping in later, so I'll get him to have a look. He has some new lotion and potions and of course the swimming pool is proving to be a real asset. I'm sure that's why we have had such a good start to the season.'

"Yes, perhaps you're right.' Charlie was deep in thought. The swimming pool was featuring much more in the horses' training regimes these days and when Alistair was here, he and Miles were often up there checking out the horses' heart rates, recovery times after exercise and so on. Then they came in and plotted everything on the computer. The swimming pool was also where Alistair kept a lot of his equipment locked in large cabinets. There seemed to be an emphasis on security and Miles had asked a handyman to install substantial new locks. If the horses were being given illicit substances in order to enhance their performance, then the stuff could be stored there. He resolved to take a look when things were quieter.

Miles went through the entries occasionally punctuated by Kim popping in with offers of tea or coffee. All seemed fairly calm after the week that they'd had, almost nondescript.

Charlie was just about to comment that he should get off and ring the police, when a car rolled into the yard. It was DI Blake.

'No racing today then sir?' DI Blake took a sip of his tea. Charlie had suggested that they go to his cottage to talk. He was wondering if the detective had made the connection between Rose Gold and the RG mentioned in the text that Will had sent to Charlie.

Think I know what's going on with RG.

'No, we don't have any runners today. So, how's the investigation going?' Charlie asked. DI Blake gave him an enigmatic smile.

'Well, we are making progress, let's just say that. Now I just wanted to ask you a few more questions. Just to clarify a few things.' DI Blake opened his notebook.

'If you remember you showed me a text sent to you by Will which said, 'Need to meet you. Think I know what's going on with RG.'' And at the time sir, you couldn't think what or whom RG might be.'

'Yes, that's right.' Charlie paused and decided that honesty was the best policy. After all he didn't actually know anything. 'Well, I half wondered if it might be Rose Gold, the winner I'd had that day. But I have no idea why he would want to talk to me about that, so I assume RG could refer to a something else, a person perhaps?'

It seemed that Charlie had stolen DI Blake's thunder in mentioning Rose Gold. He looked momentarily deflated and then recovered himself.

'Ah, Rose Gold. I was coming to that. He was your mount in the fourth race at Market Rasen. He came in at 25-1, didn't he? Rather good odds, weren't they? It seems that there were a number of bets on Rose Gold and for reasonable money too.'

'Well, his owner is the granddaughter of Caroline Regan and I imagine that might have caused something of a stir.' He shrugged.

'Really? **The** Caroline Regan, the ex Bond girl? Well, well, well.'

'Yes. That's the one. Delightful woman. She has a horse here too. You may have heard of Indian Ocean, that's her horse. She bought her granddaughter, Tara, Rose Gold as a birthday present.'

DI Blake shook his head. 'Well, some people have all the luck, sir, don't they? What's she like, this granddaughter? Is she like her grandmother at all?'

'Not really, but she's very nice actually. Rather serious. She's studying to be a psychologist. She's quite brainy.'

DI Blake rocked back in his chair and studied him. 'Well, I'll be damned.' He slowly and deliberately took a sip of tea and carefully placed the mug back on the table. 'So, this Rose Gold, did you have any reason to be surprised when he won, sir? Was it expected, unusual in anyway?'

Charlie sighed. 'Well, I had only ridden him a few times before, so I couldn't really say. He's very well bred, and he was bought by Tara's uncle Lawrence Prendergast. He's a well known bloodstock agent and has a good eye for a horse and as money is no object for Caroline, then he was bound to be a good sort. Why would I be surprised when he won?'

'Quite so, quite so sir. But I understand the Authorities did ask for a urine sample to be taken of Rose Gold after the race. Do you know why that was?'

Charlie looked into the inspector's grey eyes which were flecked with brown and green speckles. It gave him an odd, hawk like quality.

'Well, what usually happens is that the stewards pick out certain horses for testing and usually those with long odds are tested. It's purely routine and I'm sure we would have heard by now if there were any problems with the test.'

The inspector nodded and stood up to leave. 'Well, I won't keep you any further. I suppose we can ring the BHA to clarify things...'

Charlie walked him to the door.

'So, are you any further on with finding out what happened to Will? Was it an accident or suicide or ...'

DI Blake gave him a mournful look. 'O murder, do you mean? Well, we are leaving no stone unturned that's all I can say. ' He paused for a minute. 'Can you think of any reason why someone would want to murder Will Mellor?'

Even though it was something he had been thinking about, it was a shock to hear the actual words spoken out loud. Charlie thought carefully. Will had seemed to be a thoroughly normal guy with no hint of anything unusual, no dark secrets or anything like that. He was a salt of the earth type of character. He couldn't imagine that anyone would want to harm him unless he of course he had uncovered some betting conspiracy but that was all speculation, surely?

He looked the police officer fully in the eye.

'No, I can't think of any reason whatsoever.'

DI Blake nodded. 'Well, he did have rather an elevated level of alcohol in his blood, probably from the night before, so it could have been a rather nasty accident. But we have some more inquiries to make and so on.' He frowned. 'Now you seem a sensible sort of chap, someone who uses his eyes and ears. Someone who might pick up some useful information. Now if you do, then feel free to ring me about anything, anything at all.' He fished into his inner jacket and pulled out a card with his mobile telephone number on it. 'Don't forget, anything you can think of, no matter when or how trivial it may seem, please ring me.' He smiled, seemingly satisfied and waved as he left.

Charlie thought through what he had said. It seemed that the police had made the connection between RG and Rose Gold and were looking into his urine test. Failing that turning up anything, it seemed that the case would be closed. To Charlie this seemed highly unsatisfactory. He took another pain killer and decided to text Tara. He owed it to Will to find out what had happened. The swimming pool featured heavily in the training regimes, but it was the arrival of the cabinets plus their substantial locks that interested him. What on earth was in them? He decided that he ought to investigate further. He had a set of skeleton keys from a mate which he could use. The more he thought about it, the more he realised that he needed to find out just what was so important that it had to be locked away in a cabinet that only Miles and Alistair had access to.

Chapter 19

Tara sat in the room and watched Mrs Reynolds drone on and on about how badly behaved her son was. According to her, he was lazy, a liar, a thief and was the reason for the whole family's problems. His mother told them, he caused problems with the neighbours by constantly kicking his football into their garden, he fell out with the other children on the street and this in turn had set the neighbours against them and now the family felt that they might just have to move. Kyle sat next to his mother, with an expression of stoical acceptance as he listened to the long list of his misdemeanours. He seemed resigned to his fate. Meanwhile, his sister Sonia aged eight, cast him spiteful looks and huddled up to her mother as if to emphasise his isolation.

Tara was observing a family therapy session and was a part of the reflective group of three sitting in a horseshoe shape, watching and commenting amongst themselves, whilst the family therapist sat with the family and spoke to them. The family therapist was Nina, a competent and passionate woman whose neat brown bob swung back and forth as she moved her head as she spoke. Nina was tapping her foot anxiously, desperate to get Mrs Reynolds to say something positive about her son.

'But surely when you say that Kyle is badly behaved, he can't be badly behaved all the time, can he? Kyle seems to be sitting still and doing nothing out of the ordinary now, for example?'

Mrs Reynolds looked shocked, her mouth opened in surprise. She was a large blonde woman, whose hair tied back into a ponytail. She was wearing leggings and a long striped jumper. Sonia was wearing her school uniform and looked neat and tidy whilst Kyle's school shirt and jumper had seen better days and he had a long streak of mud down his trousers. His shoes were also badly scuffed and rather tatty.

Nina persisted. 'Perhaps, we should ask Kyle how he sees things, if that's alright with everyone?'

Mrs Reynolds looked shocked, as though this was not what she had signed up for. Heaven forbid that he might be allowed to have his say.

'Well, it'll all be lies anyways,' she muttered.

Kyle shrugged and looked at the floor. Nina looked at him inquiringly.

'How does it feel to be you in your family, Kyle?'

There was a long pause, then Kyle spoke. 'Well, I can't do nothing right, so I just do what I want to do. May as well. I' always in trouble, anyway.'

Mrs Reynolds snorted and was about to say something further but was silenced with a look from Nina. Tara found she had a huge lump in her throat for the boy who living with so much obvious hostility.

'And I miss my dad,' he continued in a quiet voice. 'But if I talk about him or ask to see him then *she* gets angry...'

'That's not true. You can't believe a word he says. It's his dad, what's not bothered!' Nina held up her hand to halt the conversation.

'OK, OK. We'll let Kyle finish. That was what we agreed, wasn't it, if you recall from our initial meeting. Well, thank you for sharing that, Kyle. It can't have been an easy thing to do but you have been very brave. Is there anything else you want to say at this point?' Kyle shrugged whilst Mrs Reynolds looked mutinous.

'Gosh, I'm not sure I could work with children. I felt truly awful for that poor boy,' Tara told Nina later. 'How do you manage to be so calm, I felt like screaming at her.'

Nina smiled serenely. 'Well, what you have to remember is that in families where there is a scapegoat such as Kyle, the family deal with their deep dysfunctions by blaming everything on the scapegoat. You must challenge that, slowly but surely. It's amazing how quickly things turn around sometimes. You just have to keep plugging away.'

Tara had to admit by the end of the session, mum had moved her position slightly and Kyle seemed a bit happier. It was just quite hard to deal with the brick wall of negativity that mum had built up, never mind living in that situation. She resolved to read up on family therapy processes and learn more.

Tara was meeting Callum later that day. They had seen each other a few times and he was keen to resume their previous level of intimacy. However, Tara still felt uneasy, as though Callum was still dealing with his feelings of loss and grief over his and Anna's marriage and his feelings about Alfie. She had so far resisted his advances and been quick to squirm out of his way when he tried to kiss her neck or lead her into the bedroom. She had no idea what this prolonged period of cooling off would do or how it would help in the end. But she supposed that when and if she was ready to move back the physical side of their relationship, then she would know somehow. She was surprised and pleased, however, when she received a text from Charlie suggesting they meet up. She would see him anyway on Saturday, but this sounded urgent.

Need to speak asap. How about a salad and a bottle of wine?

Tara smiled and texted Callum to rearrange things saying she had an essay to hand in and needed to work on that. She hadn't, but her curiosity about what Charlie might have to say about Rose Gold, and what it might reveal about the whole situation was overwhelming.

It was the first time that Tara had been to Charlie's cottage and she was pleasantly surprised to the find his house tasteful, rather sparse but stylish and clean. Moreover, he had whipped up a Caesar salad and steak complete with a good bottle of chianti. She had a surreptitious look round. There were a few photos of horses, Charlie as a jockey wearing an assortment of colours and holding trophies. She noticed a small photo of Charlie as a boy with a young girl, presumably his sister, but little else that suggested any lingering female presence. She found this rather surprising given his dark good looks and easy charm. She wondered if there were many women and they just didn't stay around too long? Maybe that was it?

'So, what was so important. Have you found something out?'

Charlie finished his mouthful. 'Not exactly. The police were here, and they have made the link between RG in Will's text message and Rose Gold. The detective asked a lot of questions about the betting and so on. He also said that Will had had rather a lot to drink from the previous evening, so I think they are also considering that it may have been an accident.'

Tara quelled a feeling of disappointment. She was pretty sure it wasn't.

'So, if there isn't any additional information, why the urgency?'

Charlie smiled. 'Well, apart from the obvious pleasure of your company, of course. No, I just wondered if you fancied having a look round the equine swimming pool and breaking into the cabinets in the end stable to find out what substances they are using. When Alistair is here, he and Miles are usually round the swimming pool and there is a locked cabinet in there that only they have access to. If there's anything dodgy going on, illicit substances and so on, then that's where they could be.'

Tara gasped. 'Supposing we get caught?'

'It'll be fine. Miles is usually wrapped up in his computer and headphones before bedtime and the lads should be sound asleep. And if we're caught, I'll just say you wanted to see Rose Gold or something.'

'Great, blame it all on the woman, why don't you?'

Charlie gave her a considering look. 'Well, firstly he'll just think I'm doing my duty to Caroline by speaking to you, but secondly he couldn't possibly be annoyed with an owner. You are after all his bread and butter. And as Miles often tells me, owners are king in the world of horseracing. Besides, we'll be in and out before he knows it.'

Tara looked at his blue eyes and felt all her objections fade away. She was still smarting about the fact that he considered talking to her his 'duty'. Still, she wanted to find out exactly what was going on with Rose Gold. She was the owner and therefore she was involved whether she liked it or not.

'Well, I suppose I could say I wanted to speak to you about a racing matter and then I couldn't resist a quick peek at Rosie whilst I was here. That sounds plausible.'

Charlie grinned. 'I knew I could rely on you.'

'What do we need to do?' Tara was enveloped in Charlie's black coat and was just glad she had been wearing flat boots otherwise she would have needed to borrow his wellies too. Charlie was also wearing black and was carrying a torch and a strange set of keys. They were sitting at the kitchen table waiting until midnight, when they figured all the lads and Miles would be fast asleep.

'Right. We need to get into the end stable near the pool,' he pointed to one key. 'That shouldn't be hard as I 'borrowed' a key from Miles' spare set. The awkward thing will be getting into the locked cabinet.' He followed her gaze. 'These thin keys are a set that I borrowed from a mate who did time for burglaries. He's going straight now, but he sort of hangs on to them as a souvenir, really.'

Tara raised her eyebrows and wondered about the sort of friends Charlie had. Best not ask too much, she thought. Charlie had clearly thought things through as he was wearing gloves and had a spare pair for Tara and a large plastic bag where he intended to place the evidence.

'If we are discovered the story will be that you wanted to have a quick look at Rose Gold. His stable is just nearby so it would sort of fit. Is that alright?' Charlie clearly felt the need to repeat the alibi, so it was straight in their heads.

Tara nodded. She felt quite excited in a way.

'What do we do with the bottles or whatever it is? Won't they be missed?'

'Well, I've thought of that.' Charlie dug in his pocket. 'I have made a list of common horse medicines, here look, so we don't need to bother with those.

But we'll play it by ear. If there are several bottles, packets or whatever then perhaps we will take one, but otherwise we might just need to note down the names. I have a mate in veterinary school but otherwise the internet might be just as good. Any questions?'

'Well, you seem to have thought of everything. Shall we just get on with it?'

Charlie grinned, and they made their way into the yard.

It was a clear, frosty night with only a crescent moon illuminating the yard. The whole place looked almost magical, transformed by the thin shaft of moonlight. Tara heard the rhythmic noise of horses chewing their hay and several popped their heads over their doors in surprise, blowing warm, oaty breath on them. There was the usual earthy, though not unpleasant smell of horse sweat, dung and straw. Several horses whickered as they looked out curiously, wondering if they might be fed early. Charlie spoke soothingly to them and they soon quietened down. There were in effect two yards, an older one housing twenty or so horses set in a wide arc back from the house. The second set had been built more recently and were built behind these, further from the house, with the equine swimming pool situated behind them. Tara followed Charlie watching the torchlight and trying very hard to keep her teeth from chattering and her boots from making too much noise on the concrete. She briefly looked in on Rose Gold and found him lying down, his head nodding as he dozed. Bless him! She moved away anxious not to disturb him.

Charlie had stopped by the end stable which was used to house the swimming equipment and the locked cabinets. Both the upper and bottom stable doors were closed and had special locks fitted. Charlie motioned for her to hold the torch and shine it at the lock whilst he fished in his pocket for the spare key. There was a faint click as he opened both the top and bottom doors and they both slipped in, leaving the doors slightly ajar. Charlie took the torch from Tara and swung the light around the stable which was lined with cabinets and had pegs of head collars, lunge lines, bandages and a huge bin of what turned out to be towels, presumably used to help dry the horses off when they had finished swimming. There was also a wall chart with each horse's name and the numbers and dates of their training. Most horses swam weekly but there were some who had at least three sessions per week. Charlie picked up several items, studied them then put them back. He then shone the torch at a large metal cabinet at one side of the stable and again motioned for Tara to hold the torch, whilst he fished in his pockets for his set of skeleton keys.

Charlie tried one key and gently turned it one way and then the other. That didn't work so he tried each key in turn, rotating them anticlockwise and clockwise.

'Damn,' he muttered. 'I know there is a knack to this. I'll just try them again.'

Painstakingly, he tried each of the keys again, probing and turning as he went. Tara's hand was shaking from the sheer cold as she tried to keep the torch level. She heard the sound of an owl hooting somewhere in the distance and the bark of a fox. Eventually, after what seemed like an age, Charlie tensed as the lock clicked and the cabinet swung open. Tara swung the torch beam around the neatly stacked shelves. There were packets at the top and a row of bottles and syringes at the bottom. Charlie started to lift the bottles and checked the labels. Then he started on the top shelf and did the same with the packages, painstakingly examining each box and checking the label with the list in his pocket.

'All looks legit. I've heard of most of these anyway,' he hissed. 'Best get out of here, OK?'

Damn. Tara felt disappointment wash over her. Mind you, it would just be too easy to find a neatly labelled bottle of EPO or whatever just lying around for them to find. Surely, the vet would carry anything potentially illegal around with him? It seemed so obvious now. Charlie began the laborious process of locking the cabinet which thankfully seemed a lot quicker this time around. Then, he had one last look around taking the torch from her. He dipped down to rummage in a plastic bag that had been stuffed under the towels, picked it up and motioned for Tara to follow him. In no time they were back in Charlie's cottage, the kitchen light blinding them after the darkness. Tara felt a huge sense of anti-climax.

'Never mind. I'm sure the vet will have anything potentially illegal under lock and key in the surgery, won't he? Still, it doesn't prove Rose Gold isn't being doped, does it?'

By way of answer, Charlie lifted the plastic bag and emptied the contents on to his kitchen table. Inside there were three cans of spray paint which clattered as they fell. Two of the cans had been used and had tiny spots of paint on them. The third was intact. The paint was the type used for vehicle and was a duck egg colour. There was also a jar. Tara looked on in confusion.

'I don't get it?'

Charlie gave her a triumphant look. 'Well, I think we now know that Will's death was not an accident. Look, this is the same colour as the small horse lorry and the detective asked me if Will had had a recent car accident. I can't remember seeing any sign of a bash. So, I'm guessing there was damage to his vehicle when they found him. A few days ago, we had to use the old lorry because the smaller one was in for repairs or, so Miles said.' Charlie picked up one of the cans and pointed to the colour on the side. 'This is identical to the colour of the paint work on the new lorry. So, it looks like that lorry has been repaired by someone. But why were these carefully hidden away? I think that Will was run off the road by another larger vehicle, none other than our new lorry and *they, whoever they* are tried to cover this up by repairing the vehicle themselves. Don't you see, this proves that someone in the yard murdered Will by running him off the road, presumably because he found out about the scam with Rose Gold?'

Tara tried to process what Charlie had said. She glanced at the innocuous looking paint canisters in horror. It was so much to take in.

'I'll know for certain when I check the lorry. If there are signs of recent damage that have been recently resprayed, then that proves that the lorry was involved in an accident, more than likely the one when Will was run off the road. All we have to do is find out who was driving the lorry to find the murderer.' Mick and Trevor were looking increasingly likely as suspects. But who was the brains behind the operation and what had Will found out to warrant him being silenced forever? Tara gazed at him, her eyes huge.

'So, what's in the jar?' she asked.

Charlie opened it. Inside was a cream. He gingerly sniffed it and rubbed a little onto his hand. Immediately he ran to the sink to run water over the skin which was instantly red and itchy.

'What on earth is in that stuff?' Tara peered into the jar. 'It smells like chillies or something like that.'

Charlie glanced at his hand. 'God knows. It hurts like hell, though. Almost like a burn.' They gazed at each other. It looked like it was homemade as there was no label. One thing was sure, it wasn't medication, but the very opposite. Something that would cause discomfort and burning, but to what, horses or humans?

Chapter 21

In the cold light of day, Charlie realised that the facts did not quite stack up. He couldn't inform the police yet because he wasn't absolutely sure that Will's car hadn't been damaged before the accident. Also, the lorry could have been damaged earlier and as it was a recent purchase, perhaps whoever was driving, more than likely Mick or Trevor or even Will himself, daren't tell Miles, and perhaps had tried to sort the damage out themselves? So even if there were signs of a recent repair it could be from a previous accident. Yet, all his instincts told him he was right about what had happened to Will, but sadly he felt very deflated as he knew it would not be enough on its own to prove anything conclusive. Any evidence was purely circumstantial and would never stand up in a court of law. Damn.

After morning stables and before he set off for the race meeting, he had the opportunity to ask Miles about the lorry as they sipped tea and went through the runners for the week. Kim was working through a load of invoices in the office nearby with the door open. It was amazing how she had quickly transformed the place with her competence and initiative. It was as though she had been there years rather than weeks.

'So, I see the new horse box is back, so the runners will be travelling in that, I presume?' Charlie asked, studying Miles closely.

'Yes, thank God. The old box is reliable but as slow as a boat compared to the new, nippier lorry. Mick and Trevor are just about to set off in it.'

Charlie nodded. 'What was wrong with new lorry then, shouldn't have been much being as it's hardly been used.'

'Oh, nothing, just a service or something. By the way, Kim, have we had the invoice for the new box yet?'

Kim popped her head round the door, her heavily kohled eyes appraising Charlie and smiling rather pointedly.

'Not yet, Miles. Not yet.'

There was no hint of tension or concern from Miles as he pushed his floppy fringe out of his eyes and began talking about the other runners in Indian Ocean's race. If the horse box had been involved in running Will off the road, Charlie was sure that Miles knew nothing about it. He glanced at Kim who was still hovering. She might be a very useful contact given her position in the yard. She cleaned and dealt with all the paperwork. He wondered if an invoice for the work to the lorry would, in fact, appear. Probably not, if his suspicions were correct.

Charlie set off for Haydock Park in plenty of time. It was a chilly day but thankfully the earlier showers had cleared up. As he drove up past Blackthorn Hill to take the shortcut onto the dual carriageway, a silver Audi came flying past. He had to pull into a passing place to let it pass. It had to be a bloody idiot who did not know the roads in the area, he concluded. He scowled at the driver. Bloody hell. Was that Derek Jones driving? It was someone who looked very like him. What on earth was he was doing there? Hadn't he said something about looking around the area? Well, at least by the look of it he wouldn't be racing today which was something. He wouldn't have to make conversation with the little worm. He glanced in his mirror and tried to make a note of the number plate. ADJ something, he thought, thinking that he must compare it with Derek's number plate. Perhaps, he was mistaken, he thought, as the Audi was clearly a luxury model and likely to be way out of Derek's reach.

Charlie gingerly stretched his leg in the car seat. His injuries from his fall had caused bruising but at least the swelling had been reduced by ice and he could move it quite well with only a slight twinge. His thoughts kept running over and over what he and Tara had found last night. From Miles' reaction this morning, he was pretty sure that Miles didn't know anything about what was going on. Either that or he was a very accomplished liar. It was all very confusing. Perhaps, he was just not picking up the signals because he really liked the guy and didn't want to believe that he could be involved in something so terrible? Not for the first time, his thoughts turned back to the days leading to Will's death. How he wished he had made the time to speak to Will about his concerns instead of rushing off. Trying to solve this particular problem was eating away at him, not least because he wanted to do it for Will, but also, he felt duped and annoyed that someone would dope Rose Gold. This was a horse he had ridden, and he knew as well as the next person how it might look to others and how a jockey's reputation could be easily ruined if there was any sniff of scandal or dishonesty attached to it. But who could have doped Rose Gold? When he thought about it all seemed to come back to Lawrence Prendergast. After all he had bought Rose Gold and he had recommended the appointment of Mick and Trevor. Miles had made the decision to close down the travelling side of the operation to just those two staff which meant that anything could happen on the way to the races. And Miles had done that due to information from someone about what Davy was getting up to. According to Gina that was old information anyway, as Rosie had been gone for six months. He wondered who had fed that piece of information to Miles? Could that also have been Lawrence Prendergast? Perhaps, Alistair, Lawrence, Mick and Trevor were all involved? One thing was certain. He was going to have to tread very carefully if Lawrence was implicated. Not only was he Tara's uncle, he was also a very well respected bloodstock agent.

Haydock Park was one of Charlie's favourite racecourses and Indian Ocean had previously won there so Charlie was looking forward to a good run on him. He was not at all sure about Clair de Lune who had been placed on his last outing, but prior to that had only won a couple of low quality selling races and hadn't showed a great deal of promise at home. Still, since his last outing, Miles had insisted, and entered him in a much better quality race. Glancing at the betting it looked like the punters agreed with Charlie with his odds being rather long at 15-1.

As he had guessed, Derek Jones wasn't at the meeting and it was quite a relief to be able to chat to the other lads without having to look over his shoulder. Derek made him feel quite ill at ease. He was always watchful and spent his time listening in. None of the other jockeys trusted him and he was definitely a loner. When he arrived, Tristan Davies and Jake Horton were already getting changed and the banter began mainly about the absence of the divine Caroline Regan who was still filming.

'Well, I reckon her granddaughter will do just as well,' Jake remarked. 'Bet she was thrilled when her horse won the other week, especially with those odds.' He beamed. 'Mind you I heard that there was a lot of money on that horse. I suppose it was the family. They've certainly got the dosh.'

Charlie and Tristan exchanged a look.

'Where did you hear that from?' asked Charlie as casually as he could.

'Oh, it was someone at the yard who heard it from a bookie. Think it was Gina. She's at our place now, by the way.' He gave Charlie a worried look. 'You knew she was back, didn't you?' Charlie nodded. 'Well, good luck to them, I say. The bookies usually win, so it makes a nice change for the punters to get one over them for a change,' continued Jake.

Charlie nodded. 'Which bookie was it?'

Jake gave him an amused look. 'Now don't go feeling sorry for them. They can afford it. You never see a bookie on a bike!'

That was certainly true, though Charlie who resolved to ask about to see if the bookies had any information or Gina for that matter, though he didn't relish another encounter with her after the last one.

He touched his cap to Tara in the parade ring, as they watched Indian Ocean being led round by Trevor. Tara was accompanied by her mother and uncle, none other than Lawrence Prendergast. Charlie exchanged a conspiratorial look with Tara as she spoke to Miles about the big grey's chances. He followed Lawrence's gaze as he studied the horse.

'I understand we have you to thank for our new staff, Trevor and Mick,' Charlie commented.

Lawrence looked at him in surprise. 'What? Oh, I don't know them personally, but I do know the agency where they came from. My clients have found the service from them to be very professional.' Lawrence sniffed. 'It's so hard to get good stable staff these days, but this agency is very thorough.'

'Well, they're certainly very efficient.' That at least was true. He just wasn't too sure about their honesty. 'Which agency was that, do you recall?'

Lawrence pursed his lips. 'Of course. It's called Equistaff. It's based in Epsom. Bloody good service or so I'm told.'

Charlie nodded and saw Miles approach him for instructions. His mind was in overdrive. Perhaps, Lawrence was off the hook anyway as it was quite a different matter recommending an agency rather than individuals. He made a mental note to find out who ran Equistaff for they could be crucial to finding out who had doped Rose Gold and then killed Will.

Indian Ocean seemed full of running and was just pipped at the post by a bay horse ridden by Jake Horton called Full of Guile. Indian Ocean made a bad mistake at the last fence and despite Charlie's careful riding, got right up close to the fence before taking off. Charlie was annoyed with himself initially, but then pleased that Indy managed to scramble over in one piece with Charlie still in the saddle. Fortunately, they both managed to regain their balance and finished in second by a length.

'What happened at the last?' asked Miles frowning as soon as they had finished. 'I thought we had it in the bag.'

'It was just one of those things, guv. He just decided to get right on top of the fence before taking off. Perhaps, it was the going. He usually likes it a bit softer.'

Miles nodded and seemed mollified. Charlie thought that he would never have had to explain that to his father, Nat. He would have just known instinctively.

His connections, though, and Tara were delighted and beamed as Indian Ocean was led into the winner's enclosure albeit in second place. Charlie untacked and made his way back to get weighed in. He was hoping to catch Tara, but she was chatting to her uncle who was explaining blood lines. He managed to catch her eye and she smiled probably hoping he would rescue her from one of Lawrence's monologues.

He sat out the second race and prepared to ride Clair de Lune in the third. In the parade ring the black horse was on his toes and ready for action. Charlie spoke to the breeders who were a likeable father and son combination who ran a small stud and had bred Clair de Lune. They had attended the race meeting at the invitation of the syndicate, none of whom had been able to attend.

'Well, he was never like that at home. Truth to tell, he was always as quiet as a lamb,' commented Mr Thomas, who was rather a ruddy faced farmer. He looked on in amazement. 'He was more like a lady's hack he was so quiet and mannerly. He seems like a different horse now.'

'Well, it's surprising how a horse can change when they are racing fit,' commented Miles. Charlie said nothing but realised that he had never seen this type of behaviour from the horse at home whilst in work. Sometimes, the racecourse did hype horses up but usually that was in less experienced horses who were learning their job and were still rather green. Trevor and Miles both had to stand either side of Clair de Lune and grab his bridle very firmly in order to get him to stand still so that Charlie could mount. Clair de Lune leapt off to a flying start when the tape went up and Charlie struggled to hold him. As they flew over hurdle after hurdle, it was clear that Clair de Lune was definitely in with a shout and two from home the big black gelding took a hold of the bit and pushed ahead regardless of how much Charlie tried to pull back. In the end he gave Clair de Lune his head and they pulled into the lead. Tristan Davies' rangy chestnut mare was matching Clair de Lune but put in a poor last jump over the last hurdle and never managed to regain the lost ground. So, Clair de Lune won easily by four lengths. Charlie went into the winner's enclosure to rapturous applause, especially from the punters who had bet on him at 15-1. Miles was delighted. Although outwardly Charlie smiled and accepted the congratulations, he was masking his true feelings. He felt dread ebb over him. It had happened again. The difference in Clair de Lune's behaviour and performance in this race, compared to his previous outing was just too great. This was, after all, a much better quality race and the opposition reflected that. Even taking into account, the horse's last fourth place in much more modest company, he was sure that, just like Rose Gold, something had been given to the horse to improve his performance. Since Miles had appointed both Mick and Trevor but had overall responsibility for the races the horses were entered in, then he had to be the number one suspect. Even Lawrence Prendergast was off the hook, since he had simply advocated the recruitment agency rather than Mick and Trevor individually. And after all, Miles was paying them, so they would do his bidding. As he and Miles debriefed after the race, he tried to behave normally, but he was really beginning to wonder if he was looking at the face of a murderer. The thought made him feel deeply uneasy.

Back home he remembered the recruitment company that Lawrence had mentioned, Equistaff. It had a website and was based in Epsom, the heart of the racing world. He flicked through the website and found that the manager was a Robert Smith. Charlie thought back to who he knew with that name, but he drew a blank. Perhaps the organisation was squeaky clean? There were certainly several positive reviews from a lot of trainers he had never heard of, so it was hard to check it out further without raising suspicion. He shut his laptop down, frustrated. It seemed that the jury was out on Equistaff. His doubts about Clair de Lune's performance and Miles' role in it, was altogether another question, which he hardly dared to answer.

Chapter 22

Tara was enjoying herself at the races and felt a lot more confident now she was aware of exactly what to expect, the etiquette and so on. Initially she had missed her grandmother's larger than life presence, but Lawrence was so knowledgeable that she had enjoyed chatting to him. He had an encyclopaedic knowledge of breeding and had minutely discussed Indian Ocean's bloodlines and pointed out other horses who were also by Indy's stallion, Sea God. Apparently, stallions usually passed on their speed to their offspring, but of course genetics were pretty unpredictable so whilst full siblings might look very much alike, one may not possess half the speed of the other. Tara had listened politely, hoping he wasn't going to test her on this later. Lawrence seemed to know everyone and was constantly stopping to chat to people and introduced Tara and her mother to various friends and acquaintances. It was whilst Lawrence was chatting to a middle aged man with a trilby and a rather florid complexion, that she noticed none other than Simon Norton. He was deep in conversation with a couple of other men. Since helping Charlie to break into the stable and hearing his theory on what had happened to Rose Gold and Will, she felt she should take in every detail as it might be a vital clue. One man was quite short in stature and had bleached blond hair that did not quite match his complexion and the other was a thick set man, aged about thirty. He was dressed in dark colours with close cropped dark hair. He had a lanyard around his neck and appeared to be one of the racecourse staff. Perhaps security staff, she thought, as he had the aura of a bouncer or boxer. Of someone not to be messed with. Tara vaguely recognised the blond man with the prominent eyes but could not recall where she knew him from. She studied Simon noticing how comfortable he seemed within the racing environment. He looked up and for a fraction of a second their eyes met. She smiled at him, expecting some acknowledgment, but he simply moved abruptly out of her line of vision. He was probably trying to avoid her, she realised, but then perhaps he simply hadn't registered her presence or recognised her. She felt a pang of dismay, as she needed to speak to him but then decided that her original plan to pop in with his wife's scarf, might be a better option.

As they walked to the stands to watch the race, she walked directly past Simon. He definitely saw her this time, but again turned away to continue his conversation. She smarted a little at his rudeness, but then thought that if she was in his position, she might have done the same thing. After all, she symbolised the establishment and his failure to deal with his addictive behaviour. Tara decided to report everything back to Charlie. If Simon was involved in a betting scam, then the other men might well be implicated. Then she had a brainwave. Rather than try to commit everything to memory she surreptitiously pulled out her iPhone, made sure that she had turned off the flash and took several pictures of the three men whilst she tried to fix her gaze elsewhere. She took several in succession as casually as she could. Her mother gave her a strange look.

'Tara, darling, what on earth are you doing?'

'Oh, I just don't want to miss a thing. I promised Granny I'd give her a blow by blow account of the race and send her some pics,' she lied.

'Oh, these youngsters and their technology,' commented Lawrence, indulgently. 'It seems you can do everything on a 'phone these days except ring someone.' Lawrence pulled out a very old Nokia. 'Now this is what I call a 'phone. Simple and uncomplicated.'

Tara laughed. She quickly sent the pictures to Charlie with a brief text. Glancing at the three, who were still deep in conversation, she noticed Simon give her a startled look. Perhaps, he had just worked out who she was? Well, two could play a that game. She pulled up her coat collar and ignored him. As the public address system boomed out announcing the start of the next race, she borrowed Lawrence's binoculars and trained them on the big grey ridden by Charlie in her grandmother's distinctive purple hooped colours. She tracked Indian Ocean who was doing well and in a good position after the first circuit. On the second she became increasingly animated as the big grey looked like he was going to win. Then disaster struck and there was an audible sigh from the crowd, as Indy made a mistake at the last when he misjudged the last hurdle. For a split second he looked like he was going to fall, but just about scrambled to safety. He rallied and put in a good run, coming in second after a valiant battle with Full of Guile.

'The jockey did well to hang on in there, well ridden,' announced Lawrence. 'I don't think Indy particularly likes the going. His sire was the same. Good ground would suit him much more. That Charlie Durrant is a damned good rider, though.'

Tara felt absurdly proud of Charlie and took several more photos of Indy in the winner's enclosure in second place. She could send them later to her grandmother who would no doubt be delighted.

Charlie, his face speckled in mud, apart from where his goggles had been, looked tired but pleased and explained about the mistake on the last fence.

'The ground felt very soft on the run up to the fence and he just got underneath it,' he explained in the race debrief. He turned to Miles. 'I wouldn't run him in such soft ground in the future, he just doesn't like it. But he ran pretty well, even so.'

'Quite, well done. You did well to stay in the plate, excellent riding, young man,' exclaimed Lawrence. Charlie beamed and caught Tara's eye.

'Well done, Caroline will be delighted,' Tara agreed.

Charlie grinned and having untacked went off to get weighed in. Tara, Lawrence and her mother enjoyed the rest of the day and Tara took a few more photos on her iPhone, intending to make a montage for her grandmother as she knew it was the kind of thing she would really appreciate. They cheered Charlie home on the beautiful Clair de Lune which Lawrence declared an amazing win and thoroughly enjoyed themselves.

Lawrence was delighted to have had a bet on Clair de Lune for 15-1, so was flushed and happy. Tara noticed the long odds and wondered about them but decided it probably didn't mean anything. She would ask Charlie later. Lawrence had brought them and dropped Tara and her mother off at the family home where Tara had left her car. Despite her mother trying to persuade her to join them for tea, she decided that as she was seeing Callum later, she would drive straight home.

As she drove, she went back through the events of the day in her mind. She hoped to have time to email her grandmother before she went out. She wondered if Charlie had seen her photos and whether or not it would have significance for him. As he hadn't contacted her then she guessed not. In fact, he was probably wondering why on earth she had sent it. Something about the blond man's face was vaguely familiar, his bleached hair and prominent eyes but she still couldn't quite place where she had seen him before. It was now coming up to about six and darkness had descended at about four. Although, there had been heavy rain in the last few days, it was now freezing outside. Tara turned up the heater in her car and pulled up the collar. She decided to take a detour to her house to avoid York city centre which, so close to Christmas, she knew would be bustling with people and probably gridlocked. She glanced in her mirror. There seemed to have been the same car behind her for the last few miles. The same circular yellow headlights had been visible in her mirror for ages. Was she being followed? Now she was just being fanciful. Car headlights were remarkably similar anyway. Having been out in the cold all afternoon, she was desperate to plunge into a hot bath and warm herself up. Whilst she listened to the radio, she thought back to her evening breaking and entering with Charlie and the implications of what they had found. Could someone really have murdered Will? It all sounded ridiculously far fetched when she thought about it. There were so many variables in horse racing, as she learned from spending any time with her uncle and with the checks and balances in place, it would be incredibly difficult, even impossible, to fix races. Perhaps, just as Miles had suggested, Rose Gold only decided to try on the racecourse. Perhaps, he was a bit of a diva that was all and needed the adrenaline rush of an audience to bring out the best in him, rather like Caroline who loved playing to the gallery and holding court. Probably, he was the equine equivalent, she decided. The thought amused her.

She continued to drive. The roads were blissfully empty on this route and the darkness was punctuated by Christmas lights set in large trees, some tasteful, some garish. *Father Christmas- please stop here* one sign read. It had been stuck into the front garden and illuminated by the streetlights. She wondered briefly what the children were like and pictured them flushed and tingling with excitement and anticipation on Christmas Eve, much as she and Fraser had been as children. The road took her right round the centre of York through a wide leafy area with large houses set back. It was eerily quiet and deserted. It seemed everyone had gone late night shopping, she thought, thinking that she probably just had time to do her usual Christmas splurge on the internet if she set about it this weekend. There would still be time for delivery. Her headlights picked out some road works up ahead, so she dipped her lights and slowed right down to a halt and waited. Damn, she glanced at her watch hoping that she wouldn't be too delayed. She had a hot bath and a date to look forward to and she was starting to feel a little woozy from her unaccustomed glass of wine over the lunch that Lawrence had treated them to. She sat patiently at first and then sighed and tutted in frustration, as the red light blinked but obstinately refused to change colour. Again, she waited, deciding that the temporary traffic lights must be faulty. She tried to look ahead past the lights, but the road bent sharply to the right and it was impossible to see if there was any traffic coming the other way. Damn. She daren't risk ignoring the lights and driving through anyway, as the left hand carriageway was completely cordoned off with orange and white bollards. A car pulled up behind her. Great, she thought, as she opened the car door, perhaps whoever was driving might have some bright ideas or be able to fix the lights or something. Or at least she would have someone to have a moan with who might be able to help her with a detour. She climbed out of the door into the cold and walked towards the car, deciding on a whim to take her tan Mulberry bag with her. It was a present from her grandmother, and she loved the size and capaciousness of it. She didn't want to leave it and risk it being stolen. She had half an eye on the lights just to make sure that they didn't change suddenly. That would be just her luck and then she would feel like a complete idiot. She walked about three steps towards the car, her eyes narrowing in the dark as she tried to pick out the driver in the half light. Strangely enough he didn't appear to be in his seat. Then she realised why when she felt strong arms grab her from behind. A rough hand was placed over her mouth just as she decided to scream. She felt a sharp pain in her head, as she fell to her feet and darkness descended.

Chapter 23

Charlie's brain was full of Clair de Lune's suspicious win as he drove home. The horse had been really on his toes even in the parade ring and hadn't been expected to be placed let alone win. It really did point to doping and he felt sick at the implications of this. But his conscience had been pricking at him too. Sometimes he wasn't sure what was bothering him, but this time he knew it was about the way he had left things with his mother. Perhaps, with Christmas approaching and the season of goodwill nearly upon him and all the stuff with Will, he really felt like he needed to see her. His usual tactic of blocking emotions out, pretending it wasn't there just didn't seem to be working. Nor did his other strategy of making light of everything seem to be helping very much either. He felt increasingly tense, unhappy and ill at ease.

Just contemplating the possibility of Miles' involvement in a racing scam and Will's death made him feel that all his certainties in life, his markers and assurances had been completely thrown off kilter. He had thought of Miles as upper class, a bit of a twit, if he was honest, but as thoroughly decent and honest underneath it all. Just like his father Nat. That he might have got everything completely wrong was shocking and terribly unsettling. He needed his mother's constancy, her calm logic. He needed to matter to someone, to have roots. Even though he didn't agree with her befriending the man who had killed his sister, he had to admit that she had seemed much happier than she had been in years. Who was he to deny her that? He knew his reaction to her revelations would have caused her untold pain. He felt ashamed of himself for that. He prevaricated for a while then rang her when he arrived home and arranged to visit. She sounded delighted to hear from him which made him feel even more guilty. But he had to make his peace with her. He knew that there would be a call to arms in a manner of speaking, and he knew what he had to do, and he had to be ready. It was rather like soldiers writing home before embarking on a dangerous mission, trying to make peace with loved ones. There was a gathering storm that would be unleashed any time soon. He knew that as the mystery unfolded, he would be exposing himself to great danger if his suspicions were correct.

His 'phone beeped and he realised he had had several picture messages from Tara. He glanced briefly at the text which explained that this was her gambler client with two other men. He clicked on the picture and nearly dropped the phone when he saw it and had registered what they were doing. There were several pictures of three men huddled together. In one, the smaller of the men was passing small packages to each of the other men. One of these men he now knew was Simon Norton. The other man he recognised as a racecourse official, a veterinary technician called Craig. The smaller man's face was completely obscured by the collar of his coat and the angle of the lens. But he reckoned that Tara must have seen him and would be able to give him a thorough description. He wondered what was in the packages. Was it money or drugs?

Charlie rang Tara to suggest meeting up to discuss this latest revelation, but she wasn't answering. Damn. He would just have to go it alone. First things first he showered, made himself a salad combined with a shot of Scotch. Evening stables were over, and Trevor and Mick had arrived back and put the horses away. Miles had gone out, so he decided to check out the horse lorry. He pulled on his yard boots, a warm coat and a woolly hat. The yard was blissfully quiet apart from the rhythmical sound of horses chewing and the occasional whicker from those who popped their heads out to see who was there. Charlie murmured to them and strode to the area where the vehicles were stored. It was pitch black without the yard lights on and he didn't want to draw intention to himself, so he pulled out his LED torch and turned it on. The two horse lorry was parked at the back behind the older lorry. It was a duck egg, light blue colour and given its nearly new condition he reckoned it would be easy to spot any gashes or marks. Charlie swept the torch systematically over the lorry, paying attention to the lower areas that could have made contact with a smaller vehicle like Will's Astra. He tried to imagine what could have happened to Will. The car was descending the steep hill and he imagined that the horse box had been following it and barged into Will's car forcing it off the road to the left and down into the valley. If so, he reasoned, there would be damage to the left hand side of the horse box. He shone his light methodically, flicking his eyes over the lower left hand side. It was as clean as a whistle. He ran his hand over the paint work, closing his eyes so he could concentrate on the cool feel of the metal. There was absolutely nothing unusual there. He ran through the incident again in his head. Supposing the horsebox had been driven the opposite way, so it was climbing the hill and barged into Will as he drove down. This was less likely but still a possibility. The lorry would have had to rely on the superior size and weight to push Will's car off course. In which case there would be damage to the right hand side of the vehicle. He flicked the light over this side and again felt the paintwork. It was gloriously smooth. He turned his attention to the edges at the front of the lorry which were again pristine.

He jumped as his 'phone rang out, a shrill tinny noise. Damn. He had forgotten to turn it off. He fumbled in his pocket and pressed the off button and waited for a few minutes. He could hear the blood rushing in his ears. There was silence, so he continued his search, gingerly at first but with more confidence when he realised that no one was around. It was only as he swung the torch around the front of the lorry to look at the sides again, that he noticed the front grille had been slightly broken and the number plate wasn't level. He shone his torch around the front on the lorry and ran his fingers under the grille area. Although, to the naked eye there was nothing to see, he could feel roughness and ridging which confirmed that there had been some damage to the front of the lorry. His mind went into overdrive as he imagined the crash site. All the time he had been expecting Will to have been barged off the road by a vehicle alongside him, never from the rear. That meant that Will must have been shunted off the road from behind which meant that he had met the road at a right angle. How the hell had that happened? Then it came to him. He must have been heading down to turn onto the road not actually travelling on it. There was only one track which he could have travelled down that was anywhere near the crash site, it was the only one for miles. It was the track to Blackthorn Hill Farm. Will must have been driving down there and was struck from behind. What on earth had happened there? Charlie's thoughts careered around wildly. What had Will found at Blackthorn Hill Farm that warranted killing him?

Charlie made his way back to the safety of his cottage, with one eye over his shoulder. He pulled out his 'phone and turned it on. It immediately rang out. He was surprised to find that it was Caroline Regan.

'Darling, I'm just ringing to congratulate you on dear Indy's race. It was splendid. Lawrence tells me that the silly boy made a mistake at the last and you were lucky to recover. He says it was only your fine riding that helped. Now do give me a blow by blow account. Tara was meant to send me some pictures but she's not answering her 'phone. She is alright, isn't she?'

Charlie thought this was a little strange, but perhaps she had been delayed on her way home.

'She was perfectly fine when I last saw her, and she said she wanted to speak to you.' He then went on to give her a detailed account of the race including his opinion about Indy not liking soft ground.

'Well, I don't blame him at all, poor darling. It's just like us going about in the winter without our wellington boots? Dreadful, dear boy.'

Charlie was amused by Caroline's analysis but immensely cheered. It was such a contrast to his earlier gloomy thoughts. She went on to tell him some amusing anecdotes about filming and how she loved playing around with guns and fast cars.

'Anyway, I'm sorry I didn't' answer first time, but I was busy.'

There was a pause. 'I didn't ring you before darling,' continued Caroline. 'It must have been some other woman. Now, I had better ring off and let you get back to her, hadn't I?'

Charlie said his goodbyes, amused at Caroline's assumption that women were falling over themselves to talk to him. If only she knew the truth. He wondered who the other call was from and scrolled back into his missed calls to check. It was Tara's number. He pressed the phone sign and waited for her to answer. There was a crackle as the 'phone was answered.

'Tara?' He heard someone breathing and a faint humming sound which suggested that she was travelling. 'Can you hear me? Is everything alright?'

There was silence and the call was abruptly terminated. He rang again but this time no one answered. He guessed that Tara was driving and hadn't been able to speak. He made a mental note to ring her later when his phone rang out again. This time it was Caroline and she was crying.

'Tara's been mugged, Charlie. I can't believe it. She's just being patched up at A and E.' There was a muffled sound as Caroline tried to compose herself.

'Is she alright?'

'Yes, yes. Just a bump to the head, or so I'm told.'

Charlie found that he had been holding his breath.

'Thank God for that. Tell me where she is and I'm on my way.'

'Well, I was just going to ask if you would pop and see her, darling. You know, if you could just check on her, whilst I'm away.' There was a pause.

'Only I feel a little responsible, you see? They stole her mulberry bag, you see, that I gave her as a present. I know I spoil her, but I can't help it.'

'Come on now, Caroline, you mustn't blame yourself. It could have happened to anyone.' A thought occurred to him. 'What was in her bag?'

'Oh, her purse, diary and mobile, a bit of makeup that sort of thing.' Caroline's voice was quavery. 'Who would have thought she'd be mugged for her mulberry bag? It's not even the latest one!' she wailed.

Charlie tried to reassure her as best he could. He knew though, that she was mugged for something else. It had to be because of the photos on her mobile. Someone must have realised that she had taken them. And now they would know that she had sent them to him but perhaps they didn't yet know his identity. He scrolled through the photographs Tara had sent, puzzling over their significance. At first glance they looked harmless enough, three men talking and chatting. Simon Norton, the veterinary technician, Craig and the third smaller man, photographed with his collar up passing small bundles to them. Although he couldn't see the third man's face, something nagged at his brain. There was something about his stance, the set of his shoulders that looked familiar. He would try and work it out later. He quickly emailed the photos to himself and decided to change his phone. It was too risky if the gang rang him and worked out who he was, he decided. He hunted around in an old drawer and found his old mobile complete with his old SIM card he'd used before he had changed networks. It was an old pay as you go which was just what he needed and from what he remembered it still had some credit on it. He grabbed his in car charger, intending to use it as he drove. The net was beginning to close.

Chapter 24

Tara was just about to be discharged from A and E when Charlie arrived. She was sat on a hospital bed, looking pale with her family around her, waiting for the nurse to come back with a decision about whether she could be discharged. Her head ached, and she was bewildered and rather scared. Charlie grimaced as soon as he saw her. God, she must look as bad as she felt. Her parents stood up to greet him. Tara found she was very pleased to see him.

'Caroline rang and told me about the incident,' Charlie said by way of explanation. 'How are you? What on earth happened?'

Tara explained about travelling back from the races and deciding to take the long route around York. She explained about waiting at some temporary traffic lights.

'The lights seemed to be stuck so I went to talk to the driver behind me, just to talk it through really and think about a detour. I wondered if there was another route to avoid the lights. Then someone bashed me over the head and the next thing I knew there was some kindly person standing over me and they rang the ambulance.' She remembered something quite strange. 'The funny thing is the driver in the car behind me didn't seem to be at the wheel...'

'So, do you think it was him that hit you?' Charlie asked.

'Could be I suppose. Someone grabbed me and then hit me over the head. I didn't see them, though.'

Charlie winced. 'Caroline said your handbag was taken.'

'Along with her purse, mobile and so on,' continued Kate with a disgusted snort. 'It's truly shocking. She was only trying to avoid the traffic in the city centre. I don't know what York is coming to these days.'

Jack Regan tutted, his face reddening. 'It's a damned disgrace. Tara thinks they wanted her bag. It's some designer one or other that Ma bought her. All this for a bloody handbag! I ask you!'

Charlie didn't think it was the right time to point out that it was very unlikely to be the target and that Tara's mobile was much more likely to have provoked the attack. Or more accurately what was on it.

'And there's all the bank cards to cancel and so on, so inconvenient,' continued her mother. They would have both continued in this vein were it not for a nurse coming in and addressing them. She was young, and her blonde hair was neatly piled up on her head. She had a brusque but efficient manner.

'You're fine to go home but please do not hesitate to contact us again if you experience any of the symptoms of concussion.' She handed Tara a type written sheet with an extensive list of symptoms. 'I presume you will have someone with you for the next twenty four hours? Because otherwise I'm not sure I can discharge you.'

Her father gave the nurse a stern look. 'Of course, she will be coming home with us.' He gave Tara a look that brooked no opposition. 'And the police will be coming as soon as possible.' The nurse beamed and then flushed when she noticed Charlie standing at the rear of the group. This often happened when women saw him and took in his dark good looks and blue eyes. He seemed quite oblivious to the impact he was having, Tara noted. She found she liked him even more for it.

As they made their way out into the car park, Charlie gave her a hug.

'I'll ring you. Now you take care.' He seemed to hover uncertainly, and she had the distinct impression that he wanted to speak to her. All sorts of possible reasons ran through her head. Perhaps, he had a theory about why she had been assaulted? What if it was something to do with the photos she had taken? She felt the need to have an urgent conversation with him as soon as possible. How was she going to do that? Damn she had forgotten about her mobile.

'But you won't be able to ring. My phone was stolen, remember?'

'Well, you can borrow my iPhone until we get you another,' volunteered her mother. She wrote down the number for Charlie.

Charlie gave Tara a beseeching look which only confirmed to her that he had found out something significant about the investigation. Her curiosity was aroused. It would have to wait. But it was hopeless. Her parents were not going to let anyone near her. Not tonight, at least. They were still outraged at the attack and had gone into full protective mode. Her father put his coat around her and ushered her into his car. Charlie gave her a wry smile, lifted his hand and then was gone. It was only on the way home that she realised that she had forgotten to contact Callum in all the chaos, and he would probably still be sat in the restaurant waiting for her. Somehow this didn't seem to matter too much in the grand scheme of things. She would ring him tomorrow.

'I'm sorry I couldn't contact you. When I left the races, I went the long way home and was mugged at some traffic lights. They nicked my handbag which had my 'phone in it. The rest of the evening was spent in A and E. Sorry.'

There was a pause as Callum digested what she had said.

'What? Oh my God, Tara. Are you OK? I was worried sick especially when you weren't answering your mobile. I rang it loads of times and kept getting the answer machine. I went around to your house but none of your house mates were there. I was going absolutely frantic.' She could hear him wrestling with his emotions. 'Thank God you're OK. Did you call the police? Look, can we meet up, today, if you're up to it? I just need to see that you're alright.'

'Yes. The police have been this morning and I have given a statement. They seem to think that it was an opportunistic crime and since I didn't see who hit me then it's unlikely to lead to a prosecution. 'She thought back to the young police officer who her father had well and truly torn a strip off with what her father called his decidedly 'casual attitude' to investigating the crime. Callum seemed to agree.

'Oh God, Tara. You could have been badly injured. Who is the investigating officer? Do you want me to have a word?' As Callum worked as a solicitor in criminal law, he would certainly know several policemen.

'Well, I doubt it will help. I'm not sure what the police can do.'

'Well, they at least have to try and investigate this properly. Surely there were other witnesses? They can certainly question people in the area? I do know the Superintendent. I can easily call in some favours...' continued Callum rather pompously.

'Oh, no. Let's at least give them time to make some inquiries. He did say they were going to see if they could identify any witnesses and I'm sure they will do their best.'

He really did seem upset and worried about her. Perhaps, it was time to move their relationship on to what it had been previously? Her idea had been to try and be friends whilst Callum got to grips with his emotions and decided what he really wanted. It had been a few weeks now and he consistently told her that his relationship with Anna was well and truly over. But there was still this tiny niggling feeling that he wasn't being entirely honest with her. And amidst all of this was a small boy, Alfie. She had blithely thought she could handle becoming romantically involved with a married man albeit a separated one, but since she had spoken to Alfie, he suddenly became a real child with needs, wants and rights. A real little person. She had to be sure that things had completely broken down with Anna because the consequences for all of them, but especially Alfie would be huge. Still, lots of people were separated with children these days and the older you were, the more likely you were to encounter partners with baggage that included children and needy ex partners, she reasoned.

'Fine. I'll meet you at the coffee shop on the Shambles at about half twelve? That's if I can give mum the slip. She's been panicking about me ever since as there is a slight chance that I can end up with concussion apparently. But I actually feel as right as rain.'

Callum laughed. 'Well, let me know if you can't make it. I'm not in court until two so at least we should have some time together.' There was a pause. 'I miss you, Tara. Worrying about you has made me realise how much...'

'I miss you too. I'll see you later.' She clicked off, her heart swelling. At least the incident last night had concentrated the mind. It just made you think that life was short, and you had to make the most of every day. Supposing she had been fatally injured or paralysed or something? You heard about such awful things on the news. She glanced in the mirror. She didn't look too bad even so. She had slept well and the drawn look and shadows under her eyes that had greeted her yesterday evening had all but vanished. Her head was still a bit sore but there was no real damage. She set about choosing some clothes and applying some make up. Hopefully, Charlie would ring her later, but now she wanted to focus on her relationship with Callum.

The city was bustling and very busy with it being so close to Christmas. York was a mass of colour and sparkle. There were Christmas lights everywhere and the shops were full of wonderful gifts, handmade chocolates, expensive jewellery, beautiful, spiced foods and sumptuous fabrics. There were street sellers with vats of hot soup, roasted chestnuts and even mulled wine. York was brimming with atmosphere and Christmas spirit. It was a clear but cold winter's day, and she hugged her warm coat round her as she strode up into the Shambles, pausing to look into the shops as she walked. Every so often she stopped to look around her, wondering if an assailant might leap out of the crowd. But then she gave herself a stern talking to. Lightning didn't strike in the same place twice after all. As she walked, she became more distracted by her surroundings. Tara loved the narrow, cobbled street with its tall, Elizabethan black and white timbered buildings, bowed with age. The street was so narrow, she could imagine families being able to have a conversation with their neighbours in the houses opposite. She felt that she had stepped back in time, straight into the seventeenth century. It was a magical place at the best of times, but especially at Christmas. Her spirits began to lift as she walked. She had been the victim of a nasty assault, probably an opportunistic attack, that was all. But she had survived, and everything was alright. She glanced at her watch and realised that she was early but decided to have a quick coffee before Callum joined her. She ordered a latte from a harassed looking young girl and nestled down in a seat that had just been vacated by the window, to watch the world go by. She idly fiddled with her borrowed iPhone noticing with amusement that her mother hadn't really got to grips with modern technology and hadn't downloaded any apps. She made a mental note to show her how to do this.

Her eyes flickered over the crowd and she glimpsed Callum approaching somewhere in the distance. He stood still for a moment; his handsome head bent as he chatted to someone. He smiled and dipped his head as he kissed whoever was beside him. Tara's heart was pounding as she strained her neck, trying to see who he was with. There was a group of school children in purple edged, black blazers obscuring her vision of the other person. The person he had kissed. They eventually moved off to reveal a slim, dark haired, young woman. She was gazing up at Callum with a rapt expression and was clutching several, bulging shopping bags in one hand. She had an aura of calm and sophistication about her and was good looking in a classical, slightly quirky way with high cheekbones and a strong nose. Tara's throat was dry. She instinctively knew that this was Anna. And as the woman arched her body and placed her spare arm in the small of her back, it was clear by the swell of her stomach, in her otherwise slim frame, that she was a least six or seven months pregnant. Tara felt bile rise in her throat in shock. Hand over her mouth, she squeezed through the café tables and stumbled into the street and ran as fast as she could in the opposite direction.

Chapter 25

When Charlie arrived back home, his head spinning, he walked up the path to his cottage and felt a cold chill down his spine. It was dark and there was only his external light to illuminate his property but instinctively he knew something was wrong. He fished into his pocket for his keys but realised he didn't need them as he front door had been jemmied open. He glanced round wondering if the intruders were still there. He guessed not but progressed slowly and carefully into the house. Whoever had been there, was clearly looking for something specific. In the kitchen drawers, cupboards were open, and letters and papers strewn all over. It was even worse in his living room where his sofas had been upturned, a cabinet containing DVD's had been tipped over and the coffee table drawers ripped open. It was the same in the hallway, in the cloakroom and upstairs in the bedroom. What had they been looking for? The paint canisters? He went back to the cupboard under the sink where he had placed them and picked over the debris on the floor. The canisters had gone. He had another sudden thought and rushed back to the living room. The drawer where he had placed his mobile 'phone had been pulled out and there was no sign of it now. Damn. He realised that by swapping his 'phone he had taken a gamble. He had hoped that the intruder wouldn't find out who Tara had sent the photos to. He was wrong. He had greatly underestimated his enemy. They clearly realised he was on to them and what was more they now had all the evidence he thought he was amassing to bring them to justice. And what was worse was that they had had no compunction in following Tara and bashing her on the head to steal her 'phone. He began to tidy up with a heavy heart. He would text Tara, not go into details but suggest that she stay at her parents for a few days. He was seeing his mother tomorrow before racing. Then he had some serious investigations to undertake. On his own. The sight of Tara, pale and fragile, was too much to take and he didn't want to involve her and place her at any further risk.

Charlie was acutely aware that his evidence had been stolen and he had a large field of potential suspects. At least he had had the foresight to email the picture to himself, so perhaps all wasn't lost. He made a mental checklist of the perpetrators; Lawrence Prendergast, Alistair Morgan and Miles as the brains behind the scam with Mick, Trevor, Simon Norton and the veterinary technician in the minor roles. He hated to think of Miles being implicated, but it was either that or he was simply being manipulated. Was it possible that Alistair Morgan was injecting his horses without his knowledge? And if so, then why was it necessary for Mick and Trevor to travel exclusively with the horses to the racecourse? Were they giving top up jabs en route? If so, why wasn't this being picked up in the drugs test? Is this where the veterinary technician came in? He was pretty sure most of the tasks undertaken by such staff were overseen by the BHA Vets and surely such important tests would not be undertaken by a technician? All horses racing, were ID'ed by staff before racing. This used to involve matching their markings and whorls to those on their passport. But these days all racehorses were microchipped. A chip was inserted in the neck as a foal and scanned to make sure that the horse running was the same as that entered in the race. So together with the drugs testing, security and identification process, it would be very hard to get one over on the BHA, not to mention their own security service which was set up to investigate and clean up the sport. Charlie also wondered about the damage to the horse box and the repairs that had been carried out. The situation of the damage was at the front of the grille and as before he came to the same conclusion that Will's car had been shunted over the hillside by the lorry. From the direction of the damage then it was possible that Will had been driving and met the hillside at an angle of 90 degrees. So, he could have been travelling down the track that led to Blackthorn Hill Farm. There may be other explanations for the damage, but that was certainly a plausible one. And there was the sighting of Derek Jones in the area. Was that just a coincidence? Possibly, but again possibly not. He decided to text Tara stating that everything was well and that he thought she should stay at her parents for a few days. At least she would be safely out of the way. He couldn't bear it if anything happened to her.

Prior to visiting his mother, Charlie went into the yard. He made a point of speaking to Mick and Trevor. Mick was his usual busy and chatty self and Trevor was rather taciturn. He didn't mention the break in to anyone, partly to see if anyone else mentioned something incriminating but also to give the impression that he couldn't care less. He strongly suspected Mick and Trevor being involved as heavies but glancing at their build it was fair to say he wasn't sure they were up to the job. Still, clobbering a slight woman over the head wouldn't require much in the way of brawn, he supposed. Neither behaved differently towards him, he noticed. He found it hard to act normally in front of them though, particularly as he suspected them of hitting Tara.

Alistair Morgan was around helping Miles supervise swimming and other medical tests as was the farrier Steve Britcliffe. Steve was a young, all-round good natured chap, who had a great affinity with horses and was very skilled at his job. He was in the process of fitting racing plates to Rose Gold. Charlie decided to have a quick word. Steve visited lots of yards and was usually up with the local gossip, so might know something useful, he decided.

'Now then, Steve. How's tricks?'

Steve glanced up from his anvil and hammered the shoe a little more before placing it on Rose Gold's hoof. The familiar burning smell of singed hoof reached his nostrils and Rose Gold tried to leap up a little. He was tied up and it was the smoke Charlie guessed he was afraid of as despite the burning smell, the process did not hurt the horses at all.

Instinctively, Charlie went to hold Rose Gold and murmured to him.

Steve paused. 'No, everything is going pretty well. Can't grumble. Had a winning bet on this fella so can't be bad. He's the dead spit of a horse up at Blackthorn Hill Farm though, this one. Must be the same sire, I reckon.'

Charlie's ears pricked up at the mention of Blackthorn Hill Farm, the place he intended on visiting later.

'Oh, there are horses there now, are there? Didn't think anyone had been up there in ages.'

'Yeah. There's a few. Four, last time I was there.' He continued to bash the metal into shape.

'So, who owns them?' Charlie asked as casually as he could.

Steve shrugged. 'Not sure. There's no one there when I go but get paid well for it. I presume the owners are working.'

'Aren't you even sure who owns them?'

'Nah, there's a caravan there, so someone must live there but they are well looked after, otherwise I'd be straight on to the authorities. They just tell me where to find the key under a stone or summat and the cash and I lock up as soon as I've done.'

Charlie's heart was thumping but he took a deep breath and tried to look as casual as he could.

'So, you have a mobile number, then?'

'Yeah, why do you want it?' Steve shrugged.

Charlie nodded.

'Well, if they are racehorses then perhaps, they need a jockey?'

Steve nodded. 'True. I'll give it to you later.' They went onto talk about the old trainer who lived there. Charlie occupied himself with stroking Rose

Gold's forelock. Rose Gold jerked up his handsome chestnut head, as the hammering continued. His forelock flew up as he half reared, and he was able to see the coat underneath. It was then that Charlie noticed it. Rose Gold had a single whorl under his forelock. This was a circular marking where the hair grew in different directions. He stared at his head, the enormity of the discovery sinking in. He knew perfectly well that the Rose Gold he had led at Tara's party, had a double whorl under his forelock. He had looked deliberately to see if he passed the Jack Farnham test which suggested that double whorls indicated that the horse was a good one and he knew that the horse had passed the test. That was it! Now he knew what had happened. Could it really be that simple? Or had he really worked out how 'they' had carried out the scam? He certainly had a theory and Steve had unwittingly confirmed it. To be sure he needed to go to Blackthorn Hill Farm. But he still needed to work on who 'they' were. Charlie glanced over to see Trevor come out of a stable barely ten metres away. Had he overheard the conversation? As Steve continued to hammer the shoes and the nails into Rose Gold's hooves, he decided that it was unlikely given the noise level, but he couldn't be entirely sure. He decided he didn't need the mobile 'phone number after all. He would just visit the farm later to test out his theory. But before then he intended to make peace with his mother. He glanced at his watch. It was still early, and he had time to visit before the afternoon's racing.

Barbara Durrant was really pleased to see him. She looked even brighter than she had when he had last seen her. She had done something to her hair and was wearing makeup for the first time in ages.

'Well, you look great, mum. How's the job going?'

She beamed. 'Marvellous. I am really enjoying myself.' She suddenly looked worried. 'You're not still upset about that stuff with Jimmy Bird, are you? Only I can't really avoid him with him often at the hostel in the winter, especially now it's so cold.'

Charlie had thought about this a lot. Just the guy's name caused a physical reaction, a sort of shiver of revulsion. But whatever his mother did was up to her, he supposed. He couldn't forgive Jimmy himself. He detested the man for what he had done to his sister and for surviving whilst she died. He was a coward and a deserved his miserable existence. However, he couldn't deny the change in his mother. Like it or not the hostel had given her life some purpose and with the hostel came Jimmy Bird it seemed. He had missed his mother. He tried to think what Helena would have wanted? A lively teenager, she had been desperate to grow up and impatient to live her life, much good it did her. She would certainly want them to live their lives to the full. He thought about the dangers he was facing now. He had to make peace with his mother because God knows what might happen. He cleared his throat.

'Well, it's up to you, Mum. I can't forgive him. You are a better person than me, that is for sure. But so be it. If you want to see him, help him even, I'm good with it.'

His mother smiled and dabbed her eyes. She took in his tired face.

'Now tell me what else is going on with you. I always knew when you had something on your mind even when you were a boy and you have just the same expression now.'

He sat down next to her and told her as much as he dared, including the fact that he could be implicated in the scam if he knew something and did not act. He told her about Will's death and where his car was found and about the fact that Blackthorn Hill Farm was key in some way or another. She listened, her eyes wide.

'What are you going to do?'

Suddenly, he knew. 'The right thing, of course.' Whatever the consequences, he added silently to himself.

His mother took his hands in her, her expression serious. 'Look, don't take any risks. I couldn't bear to lose you as well...'

Charlie grinned. 'Of course, Mum. I'll be fine, you'll see.' He hoped he sounded braver than he actually felt.

Chapter 26

Tara had been feeling quite well since her accident, but Callum's betrayal had set her back. So that was why he had prevaricated and the whole relationship felt wrong. She didn't for once doubt that Callum was the father of Anna's child and that as such, she had no alternative but to end the relationship. Callum had rung her many times since, as he had arrived at the café to find her not there and was unaware that she had seen Anna. She knew she was delaying an inevitable, final showdown but she literally didn't have the stomach for it. She did check to see if she had had a text from Charlie though, and she had, though he appeared to be using a different phone number. He had contacted her to say that everything was fine and that she should stay at her parents and recover. Tara was jolted out of her reverie. What on earth did that mean? When she had seen him at the hospital, he HAD been desperate to speak to her about something, she was sure of it. She had a horrible suspicion that he was just being gallant and not wanting her involved in further problems, but he was forgetting that it was her horse that had been doped and as such she was involved like it or not. Besides, she was curious as to what he had made of her photos. They must have been important to warrant her 'phone being stolen. And she really needed something else to think about. She decided to text back.

Feeling much better. Shall we meet up today?

She received a text back suggesting tomorrow later in the week. Why not today? Perhaps he really was busy, but she still had the horrible feeling that Charlie was holding out on her. Was he hoping to spare her any further pain and get on with the investigation on his own? Rather than mope about, it never did anyone any good, Tara decided to go back into her placement. Her mother was less than enthusiastic, however.

'Are you quite sure you're ready, darling? You are still looking rather pale.'

Tara knew this had rather more to do with the shock of her discovery yesterday than her attack but didn't want to talk to her mother about that. Thank God she had never introduced Callum to her parents and had kept him at arms' length recently. It still hurt, though, but as she did feel that challenging work was the universal panacea to tricky emotional issues. Self pity never helped anyone. She tried to think what her grandmother would have done in the circumstances. Probably, thrown herself into work, a new role, she decided. Then she would do the same.

'Honestly, I feel fine. Really.'

Her mother gave her a considered look. 'Well, come back here for tea, so you don't have to cook at least. Risotto, for supper?'

Tara nodded. Her mother's risotto was to die for, and Callum was unlikely to turn up at her parents as he didn't even know where they lived. And right now, that was a distinct advantage.

'You're on.'

In the office, Tara had been given another referral. This was a young man who suffered from depression because of a traumatic incident, which was the death of a friend when he was young. The referral came via a GP but there was quite a lot of details about where the young man was living, somewhere called The Lilacs. Tara scanned the referral and noticed that a Mrs Durrant was involved as his support worker. She wondered idly if this person was related to Charlie as he had mentioned that his mother had recently got a job in a caring role. However, she dismissed this as although not a common name, she couldn't just assume that everyone might be related to Charlie. She made a note of Mrs Durrant's telephone number as it was always useful to speak to the other agencies involved in the case. It was unlikely to be anything to do with Charlie's mother, she decided. But it was interesting how he had invaded her life. Tara decided to make an appointment to see her new client and considered what approach she might use. CBT probably as this had been very effective in dealing with depression.

Next up was her session with Ruth Cummings. Inevitably her thoughts were drawn to Simon Norton, her ex client who had disclosed that he had won a lot of money on Rose Gold. She wondered again what he had been up to at the races and wondered who the other men were that she had seen him with. The smaller blond one had definitely looked familiar, and she was curious to see if Charlie could shed any light on his identity. Damn. Try as she may, she wouldn't recall where she had seen him before. His hair had looked bleached, so she tried to consider what he might look like with darker hair. But that didn't help. Probably it would come to her unexpectedly as these things often did. Charlie was bound to know. She would have to wait for tomorrow now to find out. Still, she remembered that she had Simon's wife's scarf in her glove box and wondered if she should pop round to his house to drop it off. Supposing he had been involved in the attack on her, though? That might really place her in harm's way. She decided to think about it and wait until she had seen Charlie tomorrow.

As she prepared for her session with Ruth, the full horror of yesterday's revelations came back to her. She shook her head and tried to rid herself of the image of a very pregnant Anna. Was her whole relationship with Callum a complete lie? Had he even left his wife given the cosiness of the display between the two? She was quite sure that Anna knew nothing about her. She felt a surge of anger at the possibility that she had been well and truly taken in by Callum. They both had. Perhaps, he was just another man trying to have his cake and eat it? Well, she was worth so much more than that, being a bit on the side was just not her style. And she knew in her heart of hearts, there was no going back. There would be no tearful reunions this time. Anna was more than welcome to him.

Ruth Cummings arrived on time, looking relaxed and a lot happier than she had in her last session. She had her hair restyled and wore some make up. The overall effect was something of transformation.

'So how have things gone?'

Ruth beamed and was bubbling over with excitement. 'Well, very well. I have had a good think about last week's session when I was really worried about my marriage. Me and Dave have been talking more.'

Tara nodded. 'Has that helped?'

'Yes. I have explained what we have done in the sessions, so Dave understands, and he had spoken about his frustrations, too.'

'So, how did that make you feel?'

Ruth sighed. 'Like a bloody pain, actually. So, I am even more determined to deal with things.' Ruth suddenly became very animated. 'Anyway, I did manage to walk round the local shop with Dave for a bit!'

Tara was really pleased. 'How did it go?'

'Terrifying, but I kept hold of Dave's arm and after the first few steps it became easier and easier. Dave kept whispering to me and told me to breathe like we practiced. Breathe in for seven and out for eleven. Anyway, it worked. I didn't have a panic attack! That was until I came to the bananas...'

Tara beamed back. 'Well, that's amazing. I'm so pleased. What was it about the bananas that got to you, do you think?'

Ruth frowned and started to shudder at the memory. 'I heard about those poisonous spiders that sometimes get packed in with bananas and ...' Ruth started to look rather terrified. 'And that set me off again.'

Tara grinned. 'Well, at least you managed to walk round the shop.' Tara was aware that this was a real breakthrough since she knew that Dave had done most of the shopping now for years. 'I'm very impressed. That is a definite improvement, well done.'

Tara could at least understand the association between the spiders and bananas which was quite logical in a way. 'Let's unpick that and go back to what you were thinking at the time when you saw the bananas.'

Ruth began to tell her. Tara was pleased though. Now all she had to do was help Ruth consider the validity of her beliefs about the likelihood of the insects being found in the store, given the steps the supermarket would have taken prior to this to remove them. In many ways this should be easier than tackling a generalised, abstract fear and it was much more understandable. At least it took her mind off Callum and Charlie, as she applied herself to questioning Ruth further.

When Ruth had gone, she stared at her paperwork for a little longer, then on impulse rang Mrs Durrant. Tara needed to make an appointment and find out more about Jimmy, but she might also be able to quiz her about what was going on with Charlie. Something told her that things were coming to a head and that Charlie was planning on doing some investigations alone. She also realised that he could be in very great danger. He was just too macho to involve her after she had been mugged. The thought both annoyed and impressed her. Mrs Durrant answered and sounded pleasant and concerned about Jimmy Bird. He was frequently at the homeless shelter where Mrs Durrant worked, and she gave further relevant information about him. Tara made some notes and agreed to send him an appointment. She couldn't resist asking further questions.

'It's an unusual name, Durrant. Are you any relation to the jockey, Charlie?'

'Yes, he's my son. Do you know him?' She could hear the pride in his mother's voice.

Tara went on to explain about Rose Gold.

'So, you're Caroline Regan's granddaughter? Well, I'm pleased to hear from you. He's told me all about you. In fact, he was here this morning before I came on shift.'

Tara took this in and felt her mood lifting. She was absurdly pleased that he had told his mother about her. Perhaps, he might have mentioned where he was up to with the investigation, too, since she had seen him so recently.

'Listen, I don't know if he told you about the investigation that involves my horse, but the thing is since I was mugged, Charlie's decided to go it alone. I think he's worried about involving me. I'm just wondering if he said anything to you about what and where he might be going? I know it's a long shot.'

She could hear the hesitation in Mrs Durrant's voice as she weighed things up. She didn't know Tara after all.

'You see I wouldn't ask but I think he's in grave danger.'

There was a pause whilst she could hear Mrs Durrant thinking things through. Eventually, she spoke.

'Well, he mentioned the Farm, you know the Blackthorn Hill Farm where he used to ride. I think he thinks that might be the key to it all.'

So that was it. 'Thank you, Mrs Durrant. I hope to meet you soon.'

Later, on her way back home to her parents on impulse she decided to drive past Simon Norton's house having taken the address from the case files. She still had the scarf in her glove box and was intending to give it to him if an opportunity presented itself. The street was in a leafy area of York in the north of the city. The houses were nineteen thirties in style and set back from the road. Number 39 looked well maintained with two cars parked in the driveway which were nearly new, expensive models. There were no prizes for guessing how Simon's winnings had been spent, she thought. She had no idea quite what to do now she was here. If Simon hadn't been in, then maybe she could have dropped the scarf off with his wife but as he looked like he was from the number plate SN1 007. She decided to park up and have a think. If Simon left, she could pop in with the scarf and talk to his wife, but she didn't relish seeing Simon again if he had instigated the assault on her. It wasn't long before another vehicle drew up the street parked. The driver got out of the car and up to the driveway of number 39. The car was sleek and silver and looked expensive. The driver briefly walked under a streetlight, and it was then that she recognised him as the blond man she had seen Simon with at the races. Nothing new there, she thought, as she already knew that they were acquaintances. But as she watched him, she realised that something wasn't quite right. He looked furtive, walked slowly and deliberately and kept looking around him, as though he was making sure there was no-one watching. He glanced at Tara's car several times, as though considering what to do next. Could he see her from there and did he recognise her? In a panic she tried to hide her face with her hair. Damn. Still, she made a note of the number plate of the car, as this may mean something to Charlie and turned around and drove away, as fast as she could.

Chapter 27

Charlie had had a reasonable day at Wetherby. He had a second in the first race on Laura Palmer's much improved Baltic Bay. The yard's grey mare, Femme Fatale however, had run badly and felt unbalanced and lame. Sure enough, when he pulled her up there was heat and a slight swelling developing in both her cannon bones, so he figured she had sore shins and would need the vet to have a look at her.

'Damn. I'll get Alistair to call in and have a look,' suggested Miles who smoothed his fingers gently over the horse's legs and noticed Femme Fatale flinch slightly. 'Maybe anti inflammatories will do the trick or maybe Alistair has something else up his sleeve?' Femme Fatale was a young mare and been little raced as a two and three year old, but showed promise jumping, hence the decision to extend her career.

Nat had accompanied them to the races and was keen to put his views forward. 'Well, that bloody swimming pool should help, shouldn't it? You need to up her sessions in there for a bit, if you ask me.'

Miles looked a little flustered. 'Quite, a good idea. I'll add her to the swimming programme.'

Charlie took this in. It sounded like a more formalised system than he realised. More like research, in fact.

'So, are you and Alistair conducting some sort of research about the use of swimming in training, then?' Charlie thought back to when they had broken into the stable near the pool. There had been a blackboard with horses' names on it, which suggested a more formal approach.

Miles looked a little shamefaced. 'Well, not as such. In a manner of speaking. It's a way of trying to get funding.' Miles ran his fingers through his floppy fringe and smiled. 'It's quite interesting when you look at the stats. I can't go into the details because we haven't been doing it for long enough, so the findings aren't reliable yet... But the results are promising.'

Nat looked at Charlie and rolled his eyes. Charlie gave him a grim smile. He couldn't help think, though, that if Miles was more involved with the actual horses rather than seeing them simply as scientific experiments then he wouldn't have missed what was going on in his own back yard. Did it mean, that he didn't know or was it just an elaborate cover up? Smoke and mirrors? He wasn't sure. He stiffened as he anticipated what he might find out later if his suspicions were founded. He was under no illusion that he could be in real danger if he was discovered. Could he handle it?

Later that evening, Charlie ate and considered what to take on his trip to Blackthorn Hill Farm. He opted for black jeans, topped off with a black coat, woolly hat, horse nuts, a bright but small LED torch, some thin but indestructible baler twine, his set of skeleton keys and his trusty penknife. He also took his old 'phone which at least had a reasonable camera on it if he needed it. He thought about who were likely to be in the caravan and what he might need to explore further. He decided to add a small chisel and screwdriver which might also be useful. He wondered whether he ought to ring the police and tip them off or the British Horseracing Authority Integrity Staff but decided against it. He should leave that for later. What could he tell them, now? It would all sound so incredibly far fetched without more evidence. He wondered again what he might find at Blackthorn Hill Farm, acutely aware that whatever Will had found there, it had very likely got him killed.

It was a quiet calm night and about 9pm when he set off. It was chilly, and he was glad he had brought his gloves and a hat. Charlie set off on the rural road wondering if he had been heard earlier speaking to Steve. Well, if so then what would await him? The moon was a silver slice in the sky, lighting up the treetops as he drove on. He started to climb up the hill and pulled his car into a passing place way down the hill, opting to go the rest of the way on foot. He locked his car and pulled up his collar against the cold and set off up the hill, his long legs making little work of the incline. There was an eerie silence punctuated only by the sound of animals in the undergrowth, badgers, foxes and the hoot of an owl. He strode on in a determined fashion.

As he approached the gate to the farm, he cast a look over to the area where Will had come off the road, or rather been driven off. He could barely make out the foliage, but even so he felt sombre. He sent a silent prayer to whoever was watching over him, God or whoever, in the hope that he would not meet the same fate. He felt in his pocket for his torch and flicked it on as he approached the gate. He shone it over the shiny, solid lock and he lifted it to up to inspect the structure to consider what key might best fit. But before he reached in his pocket for his skeleton keys, he shone the torch around to see if there was large stone around which the key might be hidden under, bearing in mind his conversation with Steve, the farrier. He noticed a large boulder to one side of the gate and dislodged it. There was a key underneath. Charlie seized it, a shiver going down his back. It was suspiciously easy, to find the key. Too easy. So, he made a split second decision and immediately reached in his pocket for his 'phone. It was almost as though he was expected and that made him very uneasy. He thought this through and decided it was time to make a contingency plan. He sent a quick text to DI Blake asking for him to meet him within the hour at the entrance at the other end of the gallops which bordered on to the main road into Walton. He thought about involving Tara but decided against it. She had already been clobbered over the head and he didn't want to risk her being harmed again. He had the distinct advantage of knowing the layout of the farm having ridden for the previous owner and ridden out many times and knew that he could make good his escape that way. He was banking on the gallops being kept in good order because they would need to be if his theory was correct. Charlie quickly unlocked the gate and on impulse pocketed the large stone. He might need it. He found a smaller rock and relocked the gate and hid the key in roughly the same place. He didn't think any of the gang would be fooled though. They were bound to notice the smaller rock, but he had plans for the larger one. He then proceeded to walk, not directly up the drive but by the far more circumspect route which would take him behind the stables and give him the element of surprise for whoever was waiting for him. For he was now sure he was expected, and he very much doubted the welcoming committee would live up to its name.

He walked on stopping every few steps to listen out and only progressing when he felt it was safe to do so. He stepped over brambles and foliage on this route, it felt like he was trying to conquer the wilderness. Eventually, he could see the grey outline of the rear of the stables and hear the rhythmic munching of horses chewing and the shuffle of hooves as they dozed. He dived under the first stable window and then lifted his head, shining his torch through the metal grille into the startled eyes of a chestnut horse. He was identical to Rose Gold. This must be the ringer and he guessed that this Rose Gold had a double whorl unlike the real one. Moving on to the next, his light flickered on the sleeping form of the ringer for Clair de Lune, a black horse, identical to the horse at Thornley. This animal was lying down with his head up and dozing peacefully, his bottom lip relaxed and protruding. There were two more horses in the next two stables, a couple of bays that were probably going to be passed off as Fringe Benefits and Jamaica Inn, he guessed. He prowled round the side of the stable, switching off his light and pausing for a second for his eyes to become adjusted to the light. The yard looked to be how he remembered it with an expanse of concrete in front of the brick built stables. There were six in total and the end one was used as an office come tack room. He could just make out a small caravan placed to one side of the yard. There was no light on, but he knew with absolute certainty that somewhere they would be waiting for him, probably further down the driveway as they would have banked on him coming by the direct route. He reckoned he just had time to slip into the chestnut's stable and examine the lookalike properly. He needed to find another entrance which he could also use as an exit if required. He needed definitive evidence and that was the only proof he could think of. He ducked back behind the stables and examined the metal grille at the rear. It was held in place by four rusty screws. He dug in his pocket for his penknife and proceeded to unpick the screwdriver part. He tried it in the screw head. Damn, it was too small, so he dug in his pocket and fished out the large screwdriver and tried that. It fitted well and after a few false starts when the screw seemed not to want to budge, he felt it twist, removed the lower left hand screw and began work on the right hand one. This was easier, and he removed it and lifted the grille up from the bottom and leapt with one deft movement into the stable. The chestnut looked startled as well he might, so Charlie slowed down his movements and murmured to him fishing in his pockets for the horse nuts. The horse sniffed them out immediately and greedily nudged Charlie for some more.

'Here, you greedy devil.' Charlie dug out some more and by the light of his phone illuminated the horse's forehead. He lifted the forelock. There was the double whorl which categorically proved that this was not the real Rose Gold. He took a quick picture with his phone whilst keeping the horse occupied with the nuts. It was then that he heard a distant rumble and a vehicle pull into the yard, its headlights lit up the grubby caravan. The engine was turned off and he heard three car doors open and close and the low rumble of conversation.

'Better check the horses, I'll look round for him...' It was Mick's voice and he could make out a couple of other grunts and footsteps, which made three of them. Charlie guessed that one would be Trevor, Mick and he had a good idea who the third person would be. Charlie stood stock still, wondering how best to play it. Torches were swinging towards the stables. Was it all over for him? He looked around noticing that floor was generously strewn with straw, but it would hardly be enough to hide a fully grown man. His eyes scanned the stable and he remembered that these were old fashioned ones with hayracks in the corner. If he could get up above the hayrack, he might be able to climb onto the narrow ledge near the ceiling beams, but how to do that quietly? No, probably not. He could hear someone approaching but fortunately they started checking the horses from the other end of the block. He heard the bolts of the stable door being pulled back and someone moving around. He had a crazy idea, but it was so crazy it just might work. He would need a head collar. Usually the horse's head collars were kept outside their stable, could he reach the one outside the chestnut's door? He crept to the front of the stable as he heard sounds of water buckets being replenished. With one deft movement he felt for the head collar on the hook outside the door and lifted it up over towards him. He delved in his pocket for his baler twine and fixed one end to each side of the head collar fashioning reins which doubled back to form a noseband over the horse's muzzle which would tighten when pulled so as place pressure on the nose. He had to have some control over his mount for what he had planned. It was makeshift, but it would have to do. The murmurs and sounds were getting nearer so he quickly buckled the head collar into place on the chestnut's head, arranged the bright orange reins over the horse's head and muttering soothingly as he did so.

He stood to the left of the chestnut who had heard the sounds and wandered off near the door to find out what was going on. Which was just as well. They were poised for action. Timing was everything. Every nerve in his body was on red alert as he waited and waited. He felt for the large stone in his pocket. Time seemed to halt. He thought about DI Blake and wondered if he was in place because his plan depended on it. He knew though, that in his heart of hearts, he would be. It seemed to take forever for the man to reach the end stable. Then, he heard the scraping of boots on the concrete outside and the bolts on the stable door being drawn back. They were so close. As he heard the click of the switch and in an explosion of light, Charlie leap forward and threw the stone at the forehead of the man, leapt onto the chestnut's back and dug his heels into his sides. The horse leapt forward, startled into the astonished face of Derek Jones and out of the door. There was a roar from Derek as he fell back, clutching his forehead, narrowly avoiding the full weight of the horse against him as he sprang out of the stable door.

Charlie steered the horse out onto the yard, avoiding a muck pile, a wheelbarrow and various other implements and out onto the narrow piece of land towards the gallops. The horse's hooves clattered on the concrete and he was dimly aware of his enemies regrouping and starting up their Land Rover to pursue him. There were shouts and calls and a roar as they clambered into their vehicle and slithered after him. The chestnut gamely galloped forward, barely hampered by his rug and enjoying his night training. By the moonlight they navigated their way along the top of the covert which led down to the gallops and beyond to safety. In the distance he could see that the Land Rover was hurtling towards them, advancing at increasing speed. He thought he heard obscenities flying on the wind as he steered the chestnut at a trot now through the trees and down to the gallops where they could pick up speed to the rear gate where DI Blake and his reinforcements would be waiting. He hoped and prayed that they would be there. Otherwise, he might suffer the same fate as poor Will.

Charlie urged his mount forwards, as the sound of the vehicle became louder and louder, its lights brighter and brighter as it closed the gap. His long legs clung around the horse, urging him forward. The chestnut must have thought it was a strange time for a training run but ran on gamely. Thankfully, the gallops were well maintained as they soared forward, avoiding rabbit holes as they went. The bitter wind caressed his face. This was the speed he was used to on the racecourse. The speed that sadly the real Rose Gold didn't possess. Charlie could dimly see that the gate ahead, that led into the next part of the gallops was closed. Did they dare jump it in the dark, would the footing be secure enough to prevent serious injury for them both? It would be incredibly difficult without a saddle to stay on, but he figured he had little choice. He had no time to think as he looked back and saw that the Land Rover was gaining. He pressed his legs into the chestnut's side and urged him on. The horse hesitated then buoyed up by Charlie's encouragement took a giant leap over the gate. Charlie held his breath and clung to his mount's mane as they soared through the air. They landed. The horse dipped, and Charlie was nearly thrown over his head but managed to grimly hold on, legs gripping tightly around his mount, as he recovered himself. They had made it. Charlie punched the air, his heart pounding. As they approached the gate at the end, to safety, Charlie was reassured by the flashing lights and the gentle hum of waiting vehicles. He slowed down for the last few yards, confident that he had beaten them. The Land Rover had slowed down for the gang to open the gate and was now several lengths behind him. He approached the hedge and the overgrown gate to safety and pulled up, dismounting in an ignominious heap, still gripping his makeshift reins. There was an instant flurry of activity, car doors crashing open and sirens blaring as police leapt out of vehicles and out into the field to arrest the gang, who realised too late that they had been led into an ambush. DI Blake stepped out of a police car. Never had Charlie been so thrilled to see a police officer. Tara appeared out of the shadows too and ran into his arms.

'Thank God you're OK. I was so scared that something might have happened to you.'

'What are you doing here, how did you...?'

Tara grinned. 'Well, I guessed that you were holding out on me. I was so worried, I couldn't just leave it and you wouldn't answer your 'phone. So, I spoke to your mother and she told me that you thought this place might be the key. So, I came and ran into this lot.' Tara hugged him, and he held her tight. He found he rather liked her concern. It gave him some hope for the future. In fact, no time like the present. He gazed at her beautiful face and kissed her very thoroughly.

'I've been wanting to do that since I met you.'

Tara stared back at him and then kissed him. DI Blake cleared his throat and they disentangled themselves guiltily.

'So, is this Rose Gold, my Rose Gold?' Tara pointed to the chestnut horse.

Charlie sighed and shook his head. 'Now that is where it all gets rather complicated...' DI Blake gave him a meaningful look.

'Yes, Mr Durrant, sir. I'm guessing you do have some actual evidence for us, otherwise you do realise I'm in deep shit for getting the Super to agree to these arrests.' He indicated the flurry of activity where officers with torches were wrestling gang members to the floor and handcuffing them.

Charlie nodded and by way of explanation lifted up his mount's forelock and pointed to the two circular whorls. 'Don't worry. This is all the evidence you need.'

DI Blake nodded, staring intently at where Charlie was pointing.

'Go on, I'm listening.'

It was 23rd of December and Bramble House looked exquisite. It was tastefully decorated with a huge Christmas tree in the entrance hall, decorated with antique baubles in red, greens and iridescent blues. There was a huge pile of presents underneath, wrapped in brightly coloured paper, decorated with bows and ribbons. Caroline had come back from filming for the Christmas break and had been most irritated to have missed out on the real life drama at home. She had arranged a small party with the relevant parties. Tara, her parents, Miles, Nathaniel, DI Blake, Lawrence and Lola were sipping mulled wine from a huge cauldron. Platters of mince pies, turkey goujons, mini Christmas puddings and roasted chestnuts were being circulated by smart waiting staff. Tara was sat by the roaring fire piecing together the events of the last few days. There were still some parts that she didn't fully understand, and she needed Charlie and the amiable detective to explain further. There was a hush amongst the assembled guests, as Charlie walked into the room.

He took a glass of mulled wine. Caroline beamed and walked over to him.

'Here he is. The hero of the hour. Now Charlie darling, do come and tell us everything,' Caroline purred in her best Bond girl voice. 'Tara has tried to explain it all but it's rather complicated.'

Tara drank in Charlie's dark maroon shirt and dark curls. The pin up boy of National Hunt Racing looked extremely good, she had to admit. She gave him a shy smile. He winked back.

DI Blake cleared his throat and stepped forward. He had the look of a schoolboy who had wandered into these glamorous surroundings by accident. His eyes were constantly drawn to Caroline.

'Well, I can tell you that Derek Jones, Mick Richards, Trevor and Craig are all being charged with fraud, murder and assault and are currently remanded at HMP. We are working with the BHA Integrity Services, but I can say that the operation is far more extensive than we first thought.' The assembled audience looked on expectantly.

'So how did the whole scheme work?' Tara asked.

Charlie nodded. 'If I'm not mistaken the whole operation relies on spies from their recruitment firm, Equistaff. They gain employment at racing yards, look at the yard's weaknesses, how it operates and then see if they can take over the travelling side of the yard. That part is crucial to their plans.'

'So how were Mick and Trevor appointed?' Tara's gaze flickered over to Miles who was looking decidedly shamefaced.

Charlie grimaced. 'Well, it was partly my fault. The travelling head girl, Gina, left due to our relationship ending so Miles found himself in a bit of a predicament and had to appoint someone quickly.'

Miles flushed. 'But Equistaff came very highly recommended. You had heard good reports of them, hadn't you?' He looked over at Lawrence, who had the good grace to look a little shamefaced.

'Yes, yes. As you know, my business takes me round lots of yards who were all telling me the same thing. Namely how hard it was to get good staff and how this agency Equistaff had a good reputation for providing competent people at short notice.'

DI Blake nodded. 'I think many of the recommendations were made under the threat of blackmail. You see, not only are Equistaff working in yards with a view to considering using ringers, they are also gathering up information they can use against people. We are talking about expert conmen here. They worked at the yards and kept their eyes and ears open. They knew who were having affairs, who gambled and who wanted to hide their debts. A few well placed words and they were suddenly in control. We have come across lots of trainers who have been blackmailed. For example, Miles was told by Lawrence about one of his stable lads, Davy, who was said to be conducting an affair at the races with a stable girl from another yard. This paved the way for Miles to take the decision for Mick and Trevor to take over the travelling side of the yard.'

Lawrence looked furious. 'Well, I did hear those rumours and thought it was my duty to pass them on to Miles.'

DI Blake nodded. 'Can I ask who you heard the rumours from...?'

Lawrence looked sheepish. 'Well, it was from a yard I visited where Mick was working, so I presume it came from him. Were all the recommendations from Equistaff made up too?'

'Well, they did use experienced horse staff, that's true. But they were also disenchanted with the system and wanted some serious cash. The staff were good at their jobs. Unfortunately, they were also dishonest.' DI Blake explained. 'We are investigating several other yards down south. It seems the operation was quite extensive.'

Caroline was taking this in. 'So, the horses at Blackthorn Hill Farm where all superior horses...'

'...and were substituted by Mick and Trevor on the way out to the races. Except the Rose Gold presented to Tara on her birthday was actually the ringer. My guess is that the gang wanted to see if Lawrence actually noticed that the horse had been switched. He had purchased the animal after all. When he didn't, they knew their plan would work. Only I spotted that Rose Gold had a double whorl and realised the real Rose Gold had a single one. The superior lookalike was then swapped and taken off to run in the races. They had heavy bets placed on them at longer odds and the gang cleaned up. They used doubles and trebles, so the bets were spread around a bit on other horses. Then the other two horses in say a treble were withdrawn from the race and all the money went on the remaining horse, thus avoiding the bookies suspicions and trebling the gang's stake and their winnings.'

Lawrence was looking rather sheepish and Miles decidedly edgy at this point. 'But the vet has to agree that the horses were injured it wasn't just my decision to withdraw Jamaica Inn and Femme Fatale when Rose Gold won. Nobody put pressure on me, I can tell you that.' He ran his fingers through his floppy fringe, looking decidedly awkward.

Charlie nodded. 'True, but I'll bet Mick and Trevor were the ones suggesting that both horses were injured, weren't they? '

Miles nodded.

'And as Tara knows, suggestion is a very powerful thing.'

'But how did they get through the vetting? Alistair Morgan agreed they were both lame... unless he's implicated, of course...' Miles looked thoroughly dejected as this point.

DI Blake glanced at Charlie. 'We are looking into that, but we haven't found any information to say that he is.'

Charlie smiled. 'I think naive and rather inexperienced might be a kinder explanation. You see Mick and Trevor knew every trick in the book. We found chilli based rubs along with the paint canisters. These rubs not only would make the horses feel uncomfortable causing a burning sensation enough to make them temporarily lame, the skin would also be hot to the touch, so any vet examining the leg might think the leg had some heat in it. This effectively mimicked a sprain or other soft tissue injury.'

Miles looked slightly mollified and glanced at his father who was listening impassively. The extent of the scam was truly awful.

'But what about the horses at Blackthorn Hill Farm? They needed looking after and exercising too, surely? Otherwise, how did they manage to win races?' Miles asked, looking increasingly defensive and ill at ease.

Charlie nodded. 'That's where Derek Jones came in, jockey and crook. He exercised the horses and was skilled enough to know when the ringers were fit. They then planned the substitution with Mick and Trevor. I believe he had form for this sort of thing.' He looked across at DI Blake.

'Yes, that's right. Derek Jones is also known as Alun Derek Jones. He and his accomplice Bert Smith were both previously involved in a betting scam involving unfortunate people being persuaded to part with substantial amounts of money for a 'betting tips service'. They were convinced by a couple of fixed races that the betting system worked and were given two guaranteed bets as a taster before committing the rest of the considerable fee. After that they found that the so called fool proof betting system was a complete sham, by which time Smith and Jones had disappeared. Along with their money.'

So that was where she knew Derek from, thought Tara. He was the boy from the newspaper article with the older man. She hadn't recognised him because of his bleached hair. And as for Simon Norton. He was just a greedy man with a gambling problem who hoped he would find a betting system that guaranteed untold riches. Instead he had lost thousands. He was a minor player, a victim too, probably. She had to ask.

'So, Simon Norton. What happened to him?'

DI Blake warmed to his theme. 'We believe Derek Jones was going to kill him, as he had almost given the game away in his conversation with you and they were worried he would say more. Fortunately, you turned up to give his wife the scarf, and Jones got cold feet and left. He would certainly have been on their hit list, though. Jones would have undoubtedly come back to finish the job.'

Tara gasped. Well, at least she had saved him.

'So that is why Will was killed? He discovered what was going on?' Tara continued.

Charlie nodded grimly. 'Yes. He went to Blackthorn Hill Farm and found the other horses. My guess is that he followed the horse box from the yard to Blackthorn Hill for the switch. Trevor and Mick realised he knew and ran him off the road in the horse box.' Charlie looked at Miles. 'I think you'll find that the new box never went in for a service, but Mick and Trevor touched up the damage to the front. I guessed that Will's car had been damaged in the accident when DI Blake asked me about it. So, when the new lorry went in for a service and Tara and I found the paint cans hidden in the stable near the pool, I suspected Mick and Trevor. Then, when I inspected the new lorry, there was damage to the front grille paintwork which had been repainted. I just put two and two together and worked out he must have been pursued down the road from Blackthorn Hill Farm.'

There was a silence as everyone thought about Will and his death. His last act was to send Charlie the text that started the whole investigation off. At least he had justice now and could be laid to rest.

Lawrence looked ashen. 'But horses are microchipped these days and ID'ed before each race meeting, so how did they get past the racecourse vets?'

'Racecourse vets are paid to undertake those tasks and carry out routine urine and blood tests, but technicians usually do the ID'ing as it simply involves running a scanner from the horse's poll to their withers and reading the microchip number. Craig Moor, the Veterinary Technician, was bribed to give the ringers the same number as the actual horses. His work was supposed to be overseen by the vet, but it turned out that the vet liked gambling, so he was off watching the races and he didn't carry out his checks. You see, everything is fallible when human beings are involved and therefore no system can be completely fool proof if operated by them.' Charlie seemed to have thought of everything.

The atmosphere in the room was rather tense as the occupants realised the enormity of what Charlie had uncovered and some of them realised that their actions had unwittingly allowed criminals into their midst.

'Well, I want to say how sorry I am that this happened on my watch and I intend to resign. I am so sorry that my now obvious lack of experience has led to these unsavoury people being appointed. Can I just say that Charlie did approach me with his suspicions, but I didn't do him the courtesy of listening and that I truly regret.' Miles bowed his head and looked close to tears.

Caroline stepped in. 'Now Miles, don't be hasty. I believe your father and I have come up with a solution whereby you may be allowed to learn the job and serve a proper apprenticeship, which you have never had.' She raised her eyebrows meaningfully at Nat, who cleared his throat.

'Yes. Erm. Many of you may not know that Miles had a successful career as a land agent before joining the yard and came back to take over, due my health issues. It wasn't his first choice and I don't think he will admit it, but he probably felt under pressure from me to do it.' Nat waved away Miles' objections. 'So, what I'm proposing is that I come out of retirement and have the bloody bypass op, I've been so terrified about. Then we will manage the yard jointly.'

There was an approving hum from round the room and Penelope, Nat's wife beamed.

'I'm told whilst there are risks in the op, it's far less risky than it used to be. I can help Miles and whilst I recover perhaps Charlie might assist Miles, as assistant trainer, with a substantial pay award, of course?'

Caroline beamed at Charlie and clapped her hands. 'Marvellous, after all you may well want to get into training one day yourself, darling.' Charlie looked really shell shocked.

DI Blake looked steadily at Charlie. 'Well, you're going to be busy, because I believe my colleagues in the BHA Integrity Services may be wanting to avail themselves of your services also.'

Miles beamed. 'Well, it would be a solution and that's just what I need, someone with more affinity with horses. I still can't believe two horses have been substituted with ringers from my yard and I didn't even notice.' He shook his head, somewhat bewildered.

Everyone seemed be staring at Charlie who was thinking things through.

'Well, obviously I'd want to ride as much as I do currently...'

Miles nodded. 'Of course, old chap, of course.'

'And you'd let me have an equal say in decisions?'

'You can depend upon it, Charlie. I will insist.'

Charlie looked round the sea of expectant faces. It seemed rather rude to refuse, but wasn't that how he had got into this mess in the beginning, looking out for Tara and Rose Gold?

Tara gave him an encouraging look.

'Well, alright then. I'll do it.'

There was a murmur of approval and Caroline clapped. 'Marvellous, absolutely marvellous. I knew you would. Let's celebrate.'

Lola nudged Lawrence. He glanced at her.

'Yes, can I just say that I'm sorry that the real Rose Gold isn't as talented as his look alike. I will, of course offer Caroline a full refund and look around for something more suitable.' He glanced at Tara and then Caroline.

Caroline nodded. 'Well, if that is what Tara wants. I have decided I'm not going to buy any more surprise presents, I'm not sure I can cope with the consequences...'

Lawrence shrugged. 'Well, it's up to you. Have a think about it before you finally make your mind up. The offer stands indefinitely. It's the least I can do.'

DI Blake stood up to leave. 'Well, if that's everything then I best be on my way.' He did look rather reluctant to leave them, though.

Caroline smiled. 'Nonsense, Harry. Do stay for another drink, if you're not on duty, that is? It is nearly Christmas after all and there's plenty of food and champagne, so do stay. I insist.'

Tara wasn't surprised that they were on first name terms and noticed that he had taken very little persuading. She went to speak to Charlie who was sorting out matters with Miles and Nat. She had her own dilemma to resolve. She really enjoyed her stint as a racehorse owner, but perhaps there were other reasons for that, she thought, glancing at Charlie.

Her grandmother appeared at her side and nodded towards Charlie.

'What is it to be? Would you like another horse, darling?'

Charlie turned towards them. 'I know a very nice chestnut, with a proven track record who will be for sale very soon with his owners being unavoidably detained.' Tara looked baffled. 'He's the Rose Gold look alike.'

Tara brightened. 'Oh. What's his real name?'

'Serendipity.'

Caroline grinned at them both. 'How very appropriate.'

'Why? What does it mean?' asked Tara.

Caroline shook her head. 'Gracious, don't they teach you anything in school these days? And you studying for a doctorate.' She tutted. 'It means finding something whilst you were looking for something else. What you actually find is usually better than what you were seeking.' Her eyes sparkled.

Charlie looked at Tara and grinned. They had found each other. It really was very appropriate, they agreed.

Epilogue

It was Christmas morning and Charlie went to lay some flowers on Helena's grave. It was a ritual he had begun following her death. Christmas seemed the right time to think about Helena because she had adored it. He remembered them both as kids, getting as high as kites on Christmas Eve. She delighted in everything, the presents, the tree, the baubles, the food, the fun and especially everyone being together. It tore at his heart to remember. He felt for the letter he had received and re read it.

Dear Charlie,

I know I'm the last person you would want to hear from but please read this. Helena was a great kid, but she wasn't the little innocent you thought she was. Sorry if that hurts but it's true. On that terrible night, she went on and on about me taking her joy riding. She would not let up. And me trying to be the big man, said yes. It is something I will always regret. I know I should have walked away but you know how she could be? A little crazy and wild. We saw you were kissing that girl, so we snuck out and found a likely looking car. It was easy to break into and at first everything was fine. Helena was loving it, laughing and jumping about, urging me to go faster and faster. She dared me to do a ton and when I wouldn't, she kept calling me a chicken. Then she kept squawking and making me feel bad and said she'd tell everyone I was scared. And that I had been given the right surname. Ha bloody ha!

Jimmy Bird- chicken. She kept goading me, so I put me foot down and didn't see the bend and the next thing I knew we had flipped over. I don't think she felt a thing as it was her side of the car that hit the wall. I will never forget her death and my stupidity haunts me to this day.

I want to apologise to you. I know this won't bring Helena back. I know you think you could have saved her, but you couldn't. She wouldn't have listened anyway. But she always looked up to you and told me what a great brother you were. She would want you to get on with your life as you weren't responsible for her death. That was down to me alone and is something I will have to face every day of my life.

I'm sorrier than you will ever know.
Jimmy Bird

Charlie could hardly read the rest for the tears that were falling. He remembered that night at the Youth Club. He was sixteen and could go to the disco and Helena had nagged their parents, so she could come along too. They had eventually agreed on the understanding that he would look out for her. But he hadn't. He had let her down. He had been desperate to get off with Lisa bloody Marks and he had been so keen to hang around her, he had taken his eye off Helena. He was disgusted with himself. When Helena went off with Jimmy, his friends had told him, but he still wouldn't leave Lisa until it was too late. Yet, he had known that Jimmy had a bad reputation and came from the wrong part of town and was rumoured to be an accomplished car thief, even though he was only Charlie's age. But he'd still gone on to kiss Lisa and couldn't bring himself to pull away. By the time he'd come after Helena, she had already gone off with Jimmy. Bloody fool, that he was. And as for Helena. You stupid, crazy girl. What were you thinking? His first thought was to screw the letter up when it arrived, but he hadn't. He had put it away not daring to read it until today. His throat swelled. Then he re-read it and started to feel a little calmer. Just breathe, he told himself. He folded the letter up and put it in his pocket. He laid the freesias on the grave and muttered to Helena. What were you doing getting mixed up with the likes of Jimmy Bird? Was it true what he had said about her goading him to speed, urging him on? Perhaps. She always was so full of life and so eager to grow up and live it. The irony was that in her haste to grow up, she had died. He felt calmer now, less angry, just sad. They were both stupid kids. He had been irresponsible and desperate to impress Lisa, and Helena had wanted adventure. But if he was being honest with himself, he probably wouldn't have been able to stop her. Nobody could have dissuaded her from anything when she had set her heart on it. They all knew that. It was part of her character. The thought calmed him a little. For all these years he had carried this awful guilt, but now he had to move on. The graveyard was quiet apart from a few people paying their respects, arranging flowers. It was Christmas Day after all, and he could hear the church bells ringing. He walked back and pulled up his collar against the cold, edging round the gravestones back to warmth of his car.

As he approached, he noticed that there was a pure white feather on his windscreen, its edges crimped in the damp. How on earth had that got there? He removed it and felt its softness tickling his skin. He had once seen a programme about people who believed white feathers were from angels, messages from loved ones who had passed over. He had laughed about it at the time, thought they were nutters. But perhaps he was wrong. Maybe it was a message from Helena? God, he was really losing it now. But he felt strangely comforted, nonetheless. He climbed into his car and on impulse placed the feather in the glove box instead of throwing it away.

As he drove, he felt calmer and strangely lighter than he had in years, the burden of guilt was starting to lift. He thought about the day ahead. He and his mother were invited to Caroline Regan's for Christmas Day. No luvies, she had told them, just family and dear friends. Tara would be there of course, and he found himself really looking forward to seeing her again. Things were progressing rather nicely on that front. He had shied away from deep emotional relationships, but now he felt he was ready. They had already solved a major crime together and that had to count for something. He thought about the future and his role as assistant trainer and stable jockey. It wasn't going to be easy, especially trying to rein Miles in from all his 'progressive' ideas. But he found he was looking forward to the challenge and introducing some good, old fashioned horsemanship into the equation. He pulled up outside his mother's house and waited for her to pack up the gifts, mince pies and brandy butter, she had insisted on bringing. He had tried to explain that Caroline would have everything ready, but he had never seen her so happy and animated. Not since Helena died, anyway. She was working, doing something meaningful with her life and he was grateful that she had found some peace. Perhaps, they both had? As he waited, he opened the glove box and stared at the feather, contemplating its meaning, for a long, long time.

Charlie De Luca was brought up on a stud farm, where his father held a permit to train National Hunt horses, hence his lifelong passion for racing was borne. He reckons he visited most of the racecourses in England by the time he was ten. He has always loved horses but grew too tall to be a jockey. Charlie lives in rural Lincolnshire with his family and a variety of animals, including some ex-racehorses.

Charlie has written several racing thrillers which include: Rank Outsiders, Twelve in the Sixth, Making Allowances and Hoodwinked.

You can connect with Charlie via twitter; @charliedeluca8 or visit his website. Charlie is more than happy to connect with readers, so please feel free to contact him directly using the CONTACT button on the website. www.charliedeluca.co.uk

If you enjoyed this book, then please leave a review. It only needs to be a line or two, but it makes such a difference to authors.

Praise for Charlie De Luca.

'He is fast becoming my favourite author.'

'Enjoyable books which are really well plotted and keep you guessing.'

'Satisfying reads, great plots.'

Printed in Great Britain
by Amazon